Dawn _____
him behind her menu.

She'd been sneaking glances at him since they'd first met. Had he not been a man, she would have called him beautiful, but his contradictions got in the way of such a simple description. Everything looked dwarfed around him. The chair he was sitting in looked like a toy, yet he moved with grace. He had a thin top lip as though drawn with the use of a ruler, but his bottom lip was full and sensuous. She wondered if that feature annoyed him.

His eyes were a surprise. When his gaze first fell on her face she'd taken an involuntary step back. She had expected dark brown eyes, but his were light brown. They looked the color of biscuits just pulled out of the oven. However, they didn't reveal much. Not warmth or coldness—nothing. She couldn't say the same for his voice. It betrayed a number of emotions in one word. That's when she knew how to describe him. He was an opera—bold, majestic and enthralling.

DARA GIRARD's

love of stories started with listening to the imaginative tales of her immigrant parents and grandparents. At age twelve, she sent out her first manuscript. After thirteen years of rejection, she got a contract. She started writing romance because she loves the "dance" between two people falling in love. She is the author of *Table for Two, Gaining Interest, Carefree, Illusive Flame* and *The Sapphire Pendant*. Her novels are known for their humor, interesting plot twists and witty dialogue. Dara lives in Maryland.

Visit her Web site, www.daragirard.com, or write to her, P.O. Box 10345, Silver Spring, MD 20914.

DARA GIRARD

Sparks

KIMANI
ROMANCE

To Faith—Because you were there when I needed you.

 KIMANI PRESS™

ISBN-13: 978-1-58314-789-4
ISBN-10:   1-58314-789-6

SPARKS

www.kimanipress.com

Printed in U.S.A.

Dear Reader,

What happens when a man who's ready for business meets a woman who's ready for pleasure? *Sparks!*

I loved writing this story of two total opposites trying to reach a similar goal. Like her friend Simone, I wanted to see Dawn Ajani have a little more fun in her life. Enter Jordan Taylor, known for enjoying life and women. The tension between the two—Dawn, who wanted both Jordan's business and his body, and Jordan, who was determined to change his playboy ways—provided ample opportunity for me as a writer. I was able to explore these two characters, showing both their strengths and weakness, and how each grew to love the other.

I hope you enjoy my first Kimani Romance release.

Happy reading,

Dara Girard

Chapter 1

"I'm sorry about this."

Dawn Ajani smiled at the man in front of her. She thought it was better than strangling him. Lionel Redding's deep-set brown eyes looked apologetic. He had nice eyes and wore a great cologne. He smelled wonderful. It was the first thing she noticed about him beside his large size. Too bad the guy was a pig. A late afternoon sun sent pale strips of light into the room, highlighting his thinning black hair and glinting against the silver letter opener on her desk. Its pointy tip was a tempting weapon. Dawn pushed it out of reach.

"I regret having taken up so much of your time," he continued. "You have impressive credentials of course."

Dawn kept her smile, although her cheeks were beginning to ache. A *patronizing*, lying fathead.

"But I'm considering the Layton Group because they have the kind of manpower and resources I need to handle a company of my size."

Trying not to gag, Dawn nodded, making a noncommittal sound that could be mistaken for understanding.

"They have a more established reputation—"

"I am well aware of Layton's excellent reputation," she interrupted. "I helped create it."

He cleared his throat, looking uncomfortable.

Her smile grew malicious. "But of course you know all about that." Dawn leaned back in her chair and tapped her finger against the desk. She noticed her mauve nail polish was chipped and folded her hand into a fist. "I find it amazing that it took you four hours to come to that conclusion."

"Yes, well I was interested in all that you had to say."

"Really? Personally, I find it a relief that you decided not to use my services. It would likely take you half a day to decide which tax form you would like to use."

He stiffened. "Now, Ms. Ajani—"

"Please. Do not pretend that you had any intention of using my services, Mr. Redding." He opened his mouth; she held up her forefinger. He closed it. "I admit that when you first came in here I was flattered by your initial consideration, but I now know that it was all a ruse." He opened his mouth again; she narrowed her eyes. He closed it and folded his arms. "And how did I know?" She didn't allow him to answer. "Because you seemed 'unnaturally' interested in the location of my apartment, my latest vacation, and both my professional and private life. While I have no problem sharing trivial information such as whether I prefer the color blue or gray." She paused. "Incidentally, I prefer neither color, you can put that down if you find it pertinent." She gestured to the pad where he had been taking notes. "I do take offense to nosy busybodies."

His arms fell to his sides. "I wanted to know if you had any other obligations which may have affected your attention to my needs."

Dawn rested her chin in her hand. "Just how much attention do you need, Mr. Redding?" She raised her hand. "Never mind, I am not interested. If you need the kind of attention I think you do,

I'm afraid you've come to the wrong company. However, you can find such companies under the heading of Escort Services in the Yellow Pages."

His lips disappeared into his fleshy round face. He drew in his prominent chin, causing the second one to quiver. "Ms.—"

"You've wasted enough of my time and I plan to be compensated."

He widened his eyes. "You said that the first consultation was free."

"But this wasn't a consultation, was it? It was an underhanded attempt by your client to discover how well I am doing in my new business. My initial consultations take one hour, Mr. Redding. You were an exception. It wasn't hard for me to discover that you are a private investigator. To be exact, you asked a series of such inane questions I was amazed anyone running a business could be so inept."

"I won't sit here and be insulted. I—"

"Don't be. I'm complimenting you, Mr. Redding." She shook her head and laughed without humor. "For a moment there I thought I would have better progress conversing with a tree stump."

He lifted his briefcase onto his lap and opened it. "I knew working with a woman was a mistake."

He shoved his papers inside. "You become so emotional and—"

"How much did Brandon pay you to come here?"

He snapped the briefcase shut. "I don't know what you're talking about."

"Would you like me to repeat it slowly or write it down?"

His face turned an unhealthy red. "Now—"

She wagged a finger. "There's no need to get emotional, Mr. Redding, I merely asked a question."

"You—"

"How much did he pay you?"

"Nothing."

Dawn stood and came from behind the desk. "Let me frame it a different way. Will you be paid for information you didn't gather?" She leaned against the table. "Knowing Brandon, he only paid you a third of what you agreed on and will not pay you further unless you supply him with the information he wants. Now wouldn't you hate to have gone through all this trouble for nothing?"

Lionel glanced away.

"Let me help you out."

He sent her a curious glance.

"I could give you some of the information you seek, for a small fee."

"No."

She folded her arms under her breast and sighed heavily. His gaze dipped. It was a cheap trick, but she was pleased it worked. "Very well. If you don't want the juicy tidbit I could give you, that's your choice."

His face remained impassive, but his eyes lit with interest. "Juicy tidbit?"

"That is correct."

He leaned forward and lowered his voice. "Okay. It's a deal. What do you have for me?"

"So you admit that Brandon sent you to spy on me?"

"Yes."

Dawn held out her hand. He hesitated, then handed her a few bills. She counted them then folded them up. She grinned at him when he glanced at her cleavage. "No, I'm not going to put them there." He colored a bit and looked away.

She put the money in her purse. "Good. You can go now."

Lionel surged to his feet. "Wait. What about the juicy tidbit?"

Dawn opened her desk drawer and pulled out

a tangerine. "It's delicious. Enjoy." She placed it in his palm.

He stared at the tangerine, his mouth opening and closing with no sound coming out.

She walked across the room and opened the door. "Goodbye, Mr. Redding."

"You're a conniving, lying…"

She bowed as though he'd offered her a compliment. "Welcome to Washington, D.C., Mr. Redding. Good day."

After Redding left, Dawn closed the door then went over and stood by the window. She used to have a view of Wisconsin Avenue with its well-dressed people and designer cars. Not anymore. Although she did see cars: she had an unblocked view of a parking lot.

Dawn tapped a finger against the wall. She used to have everything until Brandon Layton, her then lover and business partner, had convinced the board that as vice president, she had been involved in shady deals with the company's finances. They voted her out of office within a week.

Looking out the window, she suddenly spotted a tall lanky man acting strangely. He was wearing a gray overcoat, and his reddish-brown hair stuck up all over his head—from the wind or by design she wasn't sure. He wandered around the parking lot, probably searching for his car. Dawn folded her arms then frowned at the tightness under her arms. This jacket used to fit—loosely. She took it off and tossed it over her chair. A lot of her clothes used to fit, but not anymore.

Wouldn't Brandon just love to know about the extra fifteen pounds she'd picked up since their breakup? Her slim figure had actually gotten rather curvy. She looked at the box of donuts on the table and grabbed a half-eaten one: chocolate with coconut topping. She stopped with it halfway to her mouth. She shouldn't. She should eat fruits, nuts and low-fat shakes. She should jog every morning and drink lots of water. She should really try to eat healthy.

She sighed. Dropped the donut back in the box and tossed it in the trash bin on the side of her desk. Her stomach rumbled. She could still smell the sweet scent of powdered sugar, coconut shavings and chocolate. But she would resist. She had to get into shape.

Dawn took a step back from her trash bin and turned back to the window. The man was still wandering. She opened the window. A light breeze from winter's lasting hold struck her face. From her view on the fourth floor she could see the entire lot. Perhaps she could help. She called down to him. "What does it look like?"

The man jumped and spun around looking wildly around him.

"Up here," she said waving.

He glanced up and shielded his eyes against the sun. "Yeah?"

"Your car. What does it look like?"

"I own a green Chevy."

Dawn scanned the lot. She shook her head. "I'm sorry, but I don't see any green Chevys. Perhaps you drove something else today."

The man shook his head. "I didn't drive here." He pointed to his watch. "It's supposed to be here waiting for me."

Dawn glanced at her clock. He probably meant the bus. "No, you don't catch the bus here. The stop is five blocks up the road."

"I'm not looking for the bus. I'm waiting for the Parva."

"Never heard of it. Is it a new tour company?"

"It's my spaceship. I was certain the Telkain people would meet me here today. Have you seen them? Their friends have to return and I'm going with them. They're really small, but have a laser that will shrink me so that I will be allowed to join them."

Dawn sighed. *Great. First a pig, now a nutcase.* Her theory was correct. There were no more decent men left. "Sorry, I haven't seen them."

"Do you want to? I have them right here." He opened his overcoat. She did not see the Telkain people, but she did see everything else.

Dawn ducked back inside, hitting her head on the window frame. She swore and shut the window.

Her assistant Simone Brackus peeked her head inside. Her greenish-brown eyes showed concern. "Are you okay?" she asked in a deep melodic voice that belied her petite size and delicate features.

Dawn rubbed the back of her head. "I'm not sure."

"Well?" Simone asked, waving her hands impatiently.

"We didn't get the job. Brandon hired him to snoop."

She sighed. "I knew it was too good to be true."

"I know." She looked at the stack of mail—bills mostly. If she didn't get a job soon Ajani Consulting will have to go on hiatus permanently. Brandon would love that!

"Another hard day?" Martin, the security guard, asked her as she made her way to the elevators in her apartment.

"Yes."

"Tomorrow will be better."

"Thanks." Dawn stepped into the elevator and watched the doors closed. Tomorrow would be better. It had to be.

Jordan Taylor didn't believe in ghosts until his ex-wife began to haunt him. Unfortunately, she wasn't dead yet. Not that he ever harbored any thoughts of killing her. Killing her memory would be much more satisfying. Twisting its neck until all life was gone and throwing it in a trash heap to be forgotten. Yes, that would make his life perfect. Well, almost perfect.

He stared down at his bedroom floor, watching the red glow of his digital clock pierce the shadows amid the low lamplight. It mingled with the moonlight that splashed a pale glow on the carpet. Nobody thought he knew what he was doing as the new CEO of The Medical Institute. They were right, but they didn't need to know that. And he wasn't going to tell them.

The early April breeze tapped against his window. For a moment he considered inviting it in, letting the wind's cool breath numb his body, perhaps freeze his thoughts. But he didn't move.

He drummed his fingers against the mattress as his mind betrayed him, rehashing memories he'd wanted to banish, repeating words he wanted to forget. *Do you take this woman*—Within minutes the entire vow repeated in his memory as it had for years—*for as long as you both shall live?* He wondered if other grooms looked at their beloved and suddenly felt sick.

He had looked into his ex-wife's eyes and saw the hope, commitment, and what he had mistaken for love, shining in her sweet, brown gaze and quickly pushed his doubts aside. He had willingly handed the preacher the key to his chains with two simple words: *I do*. Damn. He flexed his fingers, pushing the thought away.

A man should not be judged solely by his mistakes, and he did not plan on making any more. He was a simple, practical man and knew the best way to avoid future misjudgments was to act in a manner that prevented them.

He would never allow himself to be trampled on by a woman's ambition.

He would never find himself in a situation he could not control.

He would never be ruled by emotion.

With that criteria he was certain Maxine would never happen again.

Maxine. Even her name had power, conjuring up memories like a genie from a bottle: elusive but no less real. A simple thing—a word, a fragrance—would transport him to the death of his marriage. To the death of his dream of home and family. He shook his head in frustration. What a fool he'd been.

"Jordan?"

He had to forget and think about the business. The Medical Institute was the best way to prove that he deserved the Taylor name. With the help of Ajani Consulting he would make it one of the most renowned in the region.

"Jordan? Jordan!"

Slowly his muscles relaxed as he felt gentle kisses on his neck. He emptied his mind and gave into the soft caress. Yes, finally a brief peace. Suddenly, teeth bit in to his flesh. He leaped up, grabbing his neck.

"Ouch! What did you do that for?" He glared at Gail. She had a satisfied smirk on her face. He had been dating her for four months and that smirk was becoming a common, if not annoying, expression.

"It was the only way to get your attention," she said without apology.

He rubbed his neck then glanced at his hand. "Did you draw blood?"

She slowly licked her lips. "No, but I tried."

His anger dissolved. He fell back and let out a weary sigh.

"Jordan?"

He shook his head. "I'm sorry. When I start to think—"

"Yes, I know. There's no harm letting someone into your thoughts."

"They aren't worth sharing."

She made an impatient gesture with her hand. "Maybe. But, honey, it's no fun making love to a man whose mind isn't there." She stood up and gathered her clothes.

He watched her, his heart sinking with regret. He shouldn't let her go, but he would. He always let them go. He should jump up and grab her in his arms, say the words she wanted to hear. Ask her not to leave. Ask her to be patient with him, give him time. All he needed was time.

Gail Walters was the type of woman men held on to. Either because they wanted to or they needed to—it didn't matter the reason. They just did. She was attractive—her eyes a bewitching hazel, her skin an almost edible mocha. He smiled as he thought of the very satisfying meals he'd enjoyed throughout their acquaintance. She was kind, a rare trait in most ambitious women, and she didn't have that desperate look of a woman looking for a breeder. She was also smart. Not that it was a requirement, but it was a nice bonus.

She was good for him, someone he could hold on to—trust. Unfortunately, that wouldn't stop him from letting her go. He didn't deserve her. She deserved someone else. Someone who would be there for her. Someone who felt like a whole person instead of half of one.

Jordan sat up on his elbows and watched her pull on her sweater. "You're leaving?" It was a stupid question, but he had nothing else to say.

"Yes." Her voice was soft, resigned. She sat down on the bed and pulled on her boots.

The room was too quiet. Silence pounded in his ears. When he wasn't living in his mind, he liked to have noise around him. "Look, Gail—"

She held her hand up and looked at him, tears swimming in her eyes. His heart constricted. She spoke, her voice a whisper. "No, please don't say anything."

Fine. He wouldn't speak, but he couldn't sit there and watch her cry. He hated to see a woman cry, especially if he was the cause. He reached out and gently touched her cheek. She leaped to her feet, as though he'd burned her. She glanced around the room then looked down at him. "When's the last time you smiled, Jordan?"

He frowned. "What does that have to do with anything?"

She shrugged then grabbed her jacket. "Forget it."

"I didn't mean to hurt you, Gail."

"I know," she said quietly, looking at everything in the room but him. "That's what hurts the most." She went to the door.

He jumped out of bed and spun her around. "Gail—"

She briefly closed her eyes, tired. "Don't do this. I'm not strong enough to fight you. We both know this isn't working. I'm not the one."

He let her arms go. "The one what?"

She looked up at him, her voice soft. "The one to give you back your heart."

He lifted a brow, more amused than offended. "You think I'm heartless?"

"No. I think you're afraid of loving someone again."

His jaw twitched. "It's only been four months. You can't expect me to love you yet."

She folded her arms and leaned against the door. "I'm not even sure you like me."

"Of course I like you. You wouldn't be here otherwise."

She shook her head, her long bangs swinging back and forth. "I'm just here because you don't want to be alone. You're afraid of being alone."

"No, I—"

She placed two fingers against his lips, her voice firm. "You're afraid of being alone, but the sad thing is you already are." She let her fingers fall. "You won't allow anyone close." She turned and headed for the stairs.

He followed. "That's not true. I spend a lot of time in my head and—"

"Ignore that someone else is in the room and trying to make love to you. Do you think that's normal?"

He narrowed his eyes and held up a hand. "Just give me a minute to come up with a good response. I'm sure I have one."

Gail glanced skyward then grabbed her purse from the hall table. She opened the door.

"That's not true," he said.

She sent him a cool glance over her shoulder. "That's your big reply? Your witty comeback?"

He scratched his head, chagrined. "A minute hasn't passed yet."

"It's over, Jordan."

Her words should have hurt him. He hoped he didn't look relieved. He let his gaze fall, and his voice deepened with regret. "I know."

He listened to her heels click down the concrete steps. They stopped then came up the steps again. He could feel her looking at him, feel her considering giving him another chance. Perhaps he had played the rejected suitor too well. "If you want to try—" she began.

He met her gaze determined to look defeated, but brave. "You deserve better."

The corner of her mouth kicked up. "Right." She folded her arms. "So now who's dumping whom?"

He blinked. This was the danger with dating smart women. "You're dumping me."

She stepped closer and wrapped an arm around his neck. He could smell the peach lotion she loved to wear. "Why?"

Instinctively his arm went around her waist; perhaps they could break up tomorrow. "Because the only thing I have to offer is a fun night in bed."

She glanced down then searched his face. "Don't sell yourself short."

His voice hardened. "I wasn't."

She sighed and stepped back. "It's such a waste."

"What is?"

"Your face."

"What do you mean by that?" He rubbed his cheek. "It's served me well."

"Yes, I know. I analyze things for a living and your face is one of the best illusions I've ever seen." She raced down the steps before he could reply. "Bye," she called, then jumped in her car and drove off.

Jordan watched her drive away and out of his life. His relief slipped into guilt then annoyance. He was used to the sadness and sometimes the tears, but he hadn't expected pity. She had no right to pity him. He didn't mind being alone, he just didn't prefer it. Why deny yourself something when you had a choice?

He stared into the dark, quiet street lined with parked cars and a newly paved sidewalk. The headlights from a car coming up the drive next door caught his attention. He watched his neighbor, Lana Patterson, climb out of her red Acura. She was an attractive woman of forty-three and had tried for weeks to start up a flirtation. He had rebuffed her efforts. Not because she was older or because her son was on the police force, but because she lived next door. Definitely not affair material. When he broke up with a woman he wanted her gone. He liked things to end clean.

He waved at her, feeling in the neighborly mood. "Evening, Lana."

She looked at him and her mouth fell open. Suddenly, her face spread into an amused smile. "Hi, Jordan. Are you feeling okay?"

"I'm fine. Why?"

"You're not cold? The wind doesn't bother you?"

"No, the weather's great. I can feel spring in the air."

"Yes, I'm sure you can feel a lot of things." She laughed and went inside.

He shook his head confused by her laughter and rested his hands on his hips. That's when he knew why she was laughing. He'd forgotten to put his clothes on.

Chapter 2

When the phone rang early the next morning, Simone and Dawn stared at each other over Dawn's desk. They had spent the last few hours trying to pretend they were busy. The phones had been silent for a while.

"It could be a possible client," Simone said.

Dawn bit her lip and reached for her box of croissants then remembered she'd already had two. She knew they weren't healthier than donuts, but at least they looked it. "Or a bill collector."

The phone rang again.

"Let them leave a message," Dawn said.

Simone headed for the outer office to answer it. "I think it's a client."

Dawn sighed and glanced around her office. She once had a closet bigger than this room.

Simone's voice came over the speakerphone. "There's a call for you. Jordan Taylor from The Medical Institute."

Dawn frowned. The Medical Institute was a well-established company that trained medical personnel. Why would they call her? "You mean A Mental Interlude?"

Simone laughed. "Cute. Pick up the phone."

"Okay." She switched lines. This was probably another one of Brandon's tricks. She leaned back in her chair, resting her feet on the desk. "Dawn Ajani, how may I help you?"

"Hello. My name is Jordan Taylor. I am the new CEO of The Medical Institute. I read your ad in *Washington Business* and would be interested in using your services."

She rolled her eyes. *Sure, and I'm a five-eleven swimsuit model*. "What can I do for you, Mr. Taylor?"

"I would like to make some changes to our company's structure and I am interested in a consultation. I'd like to schedule an appointment with you right away." He hesitated. "The issues I need to deal with are rather delicate in nature."

Dawn shook her head. It was a shame he sounded so sincere. His accent wasn't that of a Washington native. It had a slow Southern quality that made her think of Indian summers and the amber color of bourbon glistening in a crystal decanter. "Of course you would. When would you like to meet?"

"Tomorrow night. You could come to my place."

"Your place." *Right. Another pig.* "Mr. Taylor, may I suggest that you continue to play this little game on your own time? There are 900 numbers available for you. I'm sure Brandon could give you plenty to choose from."

She expected him to get angry or deny it, but a thick silence seeped through the line. Dread made her skin tingle. Had she made a mistake? "Mr. Taylor?"

Eventually, he said, "I think I have the wrong number. Excuse me."

Dawn sat up and swung her legs to the ground. Her foot dislodged a stack of books, causing two to crash to the ground. "No, wait! Mr. Taylor?"

"I'm still here," he said with a note of regret.

"I am terribly sorry. No, please don't hang up. There's been a misunderstanding. I...well, there's no excuse really." *Except for the fact that I'm a moron.* " Let's try this again. Okay?" She waited. Soon the dial tone buzzed in her ear. Dawn squeezed her eyes shut and groaned. "I'm an idiot." She replaced the receiver. "Score one for Brandon." She stared at the box of croissants, then threw them away. She had to make serious changes in her life.

Dawn stood, rested her head on the window frame and saw the man from yesterday still looking for his alien friends. She probably should call the police. She rested her forehead against the cool window. Either that or join him.

Simone peeked her head inside. "Well?"

She waved a dismissive hand and groaned. "Don't ask."

The phone rang.

"I'm not here," Dawn said as Simone went to the phone. Simone answered then listened. She hit the mute button then turned to Dawn. "You'd better answer this."

"Why?"

"It's him. That Taylor guy."

Dawn lunged for the phone and hit her knee against the desk. She swore and answered in a breathless rush. "Dawn Ajani speaking. How may I help you?"

"Is this a bad time?"

Her heart raced. Yes, it was definitely him, *bourbon and hot southern nights*. She frowned. Where had that come from? "No, not at all."

"Hello. My name is Jordan Taylor. I saw your ad and would be interested in using your services."

She felt heady from his voice and the relief that followed. She fell into her chair. "Oh, I'm so glad you called back. I am terribly sorry for the mix up before. I guess I'm still recuperating from a bad meeting with a man who took up four hours of my time yesterday and I took my frustration out on you."

"Ms. Ajani—"

"When you hung up I thought, Oh great, I've lost a fantastic opportunity. Should I call back?"

"Ms. Ajani—"

"But that would be difficult because he probably has an unlisted number. So you can imagine how—"

"Ms. Ajani!"

She halted. "Yes?"

"I thought the point of my calling back was to pretend that the previous conversation didn't happen."

"Yes, of course."

"I would like to schedule a meeting," he said with exaggerated patience.

She looked at her empty calendar. "Okay. When would be convenient?"

"We can meet outside my house. There's a restaurant that is within walking distance. Parking is difficult so it's easier to walk."

"About my fee—"

"Just send me your invoice."

She pumped the air with her fist. *Money was no object.* "Okay, also—"

"I'll see you at seven tomorrow. I'll give your assistant the directions. Goodbye."

"Bye." She transferred the call to Simone. "Simone, can you please get directions from Mr. Taylor," she said then hung up. She sagged against her chair. A possible client. Time to treat herself! She looked in the trash bin and pulled out the box of croissants.

"What are you doing?"

Dawn glanced up and saw Simone staring at her with a knowing grin. She grinned back, feeling a little guilty. "We really shouldn't let good food go to waste."

Simone eagerly pulled up a side chair and sat. "So what happened?"

Dawn dropped the box back in the garbage. "I think we might have a new client. Find out all you can on The Medical Institute."

Jordan Taylor stared at the phone. Perhaps working with Ajani Consulting wasn't such a good idea. The company was small and hungry. Something he could control. He liked being in control, but based on the phone conversation he had just had, he was having second thoughts. The owner might prove difficult. He'd find out more at the meeting. Maybe even call another company to keep his options open.

His assistant Marlene Dobson knocked on the door then entered. The bracelets on her wrists and ankles clinked as she walked. He didn't think it professional to wear so much jewelry, but she'd been with the business from the beginning and he didn't want to change what worked and Marlene certainly did.

She held up a package, the gold bracelets on her brown arm clanking together. "This is for you."

"Just put it on the desk, thanks."

He looked at the second name on the list. Franklin Enterprises, a renowned consulting firm

might have more experience. The phone rang. He
hit the speakerphone. "Taylor."

A female voice came on the line. "Hey, baby.
Guess what I plan to do to you tonight."

Jordan grabbed the phone and sent Marlene a
smile. She pretended not to notice as she put the
packet in his in-box. She left and closed the door.

"I'm at work, Gail," he warned in a low voice.

"So? You didn't mind my messages before."

"I wasn't in this position before."

He glanced around the large office both proud
and scared of his new responsibility. Only three
weeks ago he was snorkeling in Barbados until
his father decided to semiretire, because of a di-
agnosed heart condition, and made him head of
the Institute.

"What should I wear tonight?"

Jordan put a big question mark against Ajani
Consulting. "What's happening tonight?"

Her tone sharpened. "Nothing if you keep up
that attitude."

"Gail, I have a lot on my mind. What are you
talking about?"

"I've decided that we should make up. I know
you're under a lot of pressure and need space so
I think—"

"Gail. I like you. You deserve better. Honey,

you know you do. Any time you want to talk, you know how to reach me."

"Somehow this still feels like you're dumping me."

"No. Remember you're dumping me, your absentminded, single-focused boyfriend."

She hesitated. "But you're so sincere and sweet."

"I'm not sweet and you think I'm heartless, remember?"

She sighed. "That's what I tell myself, but I know better. I wish I could hate you."

"I could come up with a reason if you give me a chance."

Gail sighed again, this time resigned. "Bye, Jordan."

"Bye, honey." He absently replaced the receiver and placed another question mark on the paper next to Ajani Consulting. The owner really sounded ditzy. Perhaps he should cancel.

Someone knocked on the door. Jordan glanced up. "Come in."

His half brother Ray entered the room with a sense of entitlement Jordan was trying to achieve. Ray had been with the company since his midteens. "Have you looked at the document Revis Technologies sent?"

Jordan glanced at the package. "No, not yet."

Ray lifted the packet Marlene had placed in the in-box. "Here it is."

"Marlene just put it there."

Ray tucked it under his arm and turned to the door. "I'll take care of it."

"No, you won't."

Ray spun around and laughed as though Jordan had made a joke. "Trust me. I'll take care of it. I doubt you'd understand it."

Jordan held out his hand. "Here's a news flash. I know how to read."

"But there's nothing in here about water temperature."

"Put it back, Ray."

"You don't belong here, Jordan. No matter how much you try to play the game. You've never belonged because—" He stopped.

"Because I'm the bastard and you're not? Yeah. I can be a bastard in more ways than one so I suggest you put that package back and go on your lunch break."

Ray tossed the file down, causing papers to fall to the ground, then left.

Jordan watched the door close then sighed and picked up the fallen papers. He'd make this company work. He'd show them that he didn't take the Taylor name for granted.

His intercom buzzed and Marlene's voice came on the line. "Uh, Mr. Taylor. There's someone on the line who says she has to speak to you."

"Who?"

"She says her name is Maxine."

His gut clenched. What the hell would she want with him? "Tell her I'm not here." He pressed the button and leaned back for a moment wishing that were true.

Chapter 3

"Jordan Taylor. That sounds like a nice name," Simone said, looking at the information on her desk. Jordan had sent them an outline of his ideas to see if Dawn could come up with something for their meeting.

Dawn tapped her desk with impatience and sent her assistant a cool look. "That's not why I plan to work with him."

Simone set the paper down. "Are you sure you can do this? It's a big job. You've never dealt with this kind of assignment before."

Dawn glanced around her office at her particle

board furniture and stained brown carpet. She would do anything to rebuild her life and get herself out of this place. "Am I sure that I can make The Medical Institute a viable entity? Of course. I have no doubt that I can make The Medical Institute number one in the state. I can make it a place where people in the medical profession go to first when they want to recruit medical and dental assistants and secretaries."

"Remember it's *his* institute not yours," Simone said with caution.

"It will be our institute, eventually. A joint effort. I plan to make it very clear that it will be in his best interest to follow my suggestions."

"How?"

Dawn smiled faintly. "As long as you make a man believe something is his idea, he will go along with it."

"I'm not questioning your skill," Simone said quickly, knowing how determined her boss and friend was. "I just think, perhaps…sometimes you tend to overwhelm people."

Dawn raised her eyebrows. "Have there been complaints?"

"No, just…" She waved her hands, trying to grasp the right explanation. "People want to feel that their ideas are being acknowledged. I know that you're good at what you do and you always get results, but you also need to let others be good at what they do."

"They're obviously not very good at what they do, if they have to come to me."

"They want a consultation, not an overhaul. At times your ideas are very grandiose and that makes some people nervous. Perhaps you could start small and then build from there."

Dawn abruptly stopped tapping the desk. "I don't have the patience to start small. Especially when given the opportunity to do otherwise."

Simone nodded, but Dawn knew her friend would never understand her drive. Right now she was struggling, but she knew she would eventually prosper, and when she was strong enough, she'd crush the Layton Group.

"Basing a business on revenge is not a good idea."

Dawn's dark eyes focused on Simone. "What do you mean?"

Simone touched the information sheet. "This is about Brandon, isn't it? Everything you do is."

She stood, suddenly feeling restless. "No. This is about business. Besides I'm glad he's gone. He was a dreadful business partner. I know he has to resist lifting his leg every time he passes a fire hydrant."

"Careful. You're beginning to sound bitter."

She went to the window and glanced down at the parking lot. "I might as well get it out of my system. I need the skill and patience to handle Mr. Taylor properly."

"I doubt Mr. Taylor would like to be 'handled.'"

Dawn turned to her and leaned against the windowsill. "I've learned a lot about men over the years. They usually don't know what they want until you tell them. Well, in the case of Jordan Taylor, I'll tell him what he wants then help him get it."

"So who's next?" David Watkins asked Jordan as they sat in an upscale eatery finishing a hearty breakfast. They were both large men with appetites to match. The plates between them threatened to cause an avalanche that neither noticed. David leaned over his plate as he cut his omelet, his brown dreadlocks falling forward.

Jordan glanced at his friend, wishing he could convince him to tie his hair back. He dashed hot pepper on his poached eggs instead. "Next for what?"

"In line. Since you and Gail broke up I'm sure

there's someone new." He glanced at his watch. "Naturally, I'm not surprised."

"What do you mean?"

"It's April. Gail reached her four-month mark. Her sell-by date had expired."

Jordan scowled at his accuracy. "It isn't like that."

"Since your divorce you haven't been with a woman longer than four months."

Jordan tucked into his eggs. "You've been keeping track?"

"Three women in the last year. Does that ring a bell?"

He sipped his coffee and shrugged.

"Based on those facts the most logical question is: Who's next?"

"Nobody."

"There has to be somebody. Since ninth grade you've always had a girlfriend."

The waitress approached the table. Her long black hair hung in a ponytail, leaving her heart-shaped face prominent and displaying streaks of rouge from her chin to her cheek. "Are you enjoying your meal?" she asked.

Jordan nodded. "Yes, thank you."

"Would you like me to refill your coffee?"

He covered his mug. Coffee brimmed to the rim. "No, thanks."

She smiled and left.

David rubbed his eyes. "Either I'm suffering from déjà vu or that's the fifth time she's come over here."

Jordan watched her take an order from a young couple cooing at their baby. "She's just very attentive."

"Yes, on catching a man." David followed his gaze. "Careful, these women have nets."

"I don't plan on getting caught."

"You were once."

Jordan tapped the rim of his mug. "Yes, I'd managed to forget my three-year marriage. Thanks for reminding me."

David ignored his sarcasm. "It was inevitable. You'll get caught again too. You can't be without a woman longer than a week."

Jordan looked annoyed. "Of course I can. I just like their company. Women intrigue me."

"Until you get antsy and need to get rid of them."

"I don't get rid of them. I give them a reason to get rid of me."

David lifted a brow. "So you admit there's a method to all this."

"I don't admit a thing."

"What will you do when a woman doesn't want to get rid of you?"

He smiled. "Not a problem. They always do."

"That's not something to brag about."

His smile fell. "I wasn't bragging. It's a fact."

They were silent then David said, "You shouldn't be afraid."

Jordan gripped his fork. There was that damn word again. *Afraid*. "Of what?"

"Marriage."

"I'm not afraid of marriage," he mumbled. "I just don't like wives."

"Is that supposed to make sense?"

Jordan leaned forward, lowering his voice. "Women are very clever. They don't let us know about this transformation period they go through when you put a ring on their finger. It starts out slowly during the engagement. She becomes this pre-wedding banshee from hell, crying over lace tablecloths and napkins and screaming over whether you should have an ice sculpture of a swan or a rose."

Jordan held a hand over his heart. "But you ignore this change because you know the wedding day is a special time for her and she's under a lot of stress. Then you get married. The day when the engagement ring and the wedding ring meet. In the distance you can hear the door of your prison closing, but still you don't know what lies ahead. You've bought into the fantasy that surrounds you, the lies you've been told. You look into her eyes and she still looks the same. She still looks like the woman you've been dating for over a year. Your girlfriend. Your sweet, sexy, loving girlfriend." His hand fell to the table, rattling the dishes. "But the truth is your girlfriend is dead. Gone forever. You now have a wife."

David shrugged. "So? Isn't that the point of a wedding?"

"One day you'll wake up, preferably after the honeymoon, it will be awkward otherwise, and you'll see her looking at you. You won't recognize the look at first because she's never worn it before. However, you'll know it's not good."

"How?"

"The hair on the back of your neck will itch. Suddenly, you'll recognize it as the look your mother gave you when you did something wrong, but you weren't sure what."

David shivered. "I hated that look."

"Exactly, and that's when you'll know."

"Know what?"

"That she's going to try and change you. She's going to tell you how to wash dishes, clothes, take out the trash, what to wear, what to eat, how to shop. If you even glance at another woman she'll think you're on the verge of an affair. Once she has you suitably castrated—I mean domesticated—she'll deliver the next blow."

David scooped up his eggs, but they promptly dropped back to his plate. "Blow?"

Jordan sipped his coffee then set it down. "Yes, blow." He hesitated. "Are you sure you want to hear this?"

"Just say it."

"If you even hint at wanting to start a family, she'll accuse you of trying to stop her career, wanting to make her barefoot and pregnant and keeping her tied to the house. Don't even try to explain that you can afford for her to be a stay-at-home mom. She's an independent woman. She doesn't need to be kept and offered an allowance from some chauvinistic, egotistic…"

David set his fork down, suppressing a grin. "You're digressing."

"Right. Anyway, if you do find a woman who won't mind being a stay-at-home mother, you're still in the danger zone."

"What zone is that?"

"Resentment. You don't even know you've stepped into it until it blows up in your face. One moment she's a happy wife and mother. The next moment she blames you for all the ill in the world and hates you for looking down on her. For denying her a career of her own. She's bored, she feels stifled and unappreciated for all the sacrifices she has made." He cut his pancakes. "With those two choices in front of me, I've decided to stay single."

David shook his head. "All women are not like that."

"I agree. There are exceptions."

"See?"

"They're called lesbians."

David shook his head again.

"You show me a happily married man and I'll show you a woman with brass balls in her handbag."

"I don't believe you."

"You've never been married." Jordan pointed his fork at him. "You still have time to dream. Go ahead and take the plunge. I already have and I don't plan to again. I'd rather have a girlfriend than a wife. You get everything without the crap."

"You're paranoid."

"Think of it as healthy skepticism. I've made a study of this and I have an over-fifty-percent divorce rate to back up my claim. Think about it."

"I don't want to think about it. There are women who make great wives."

Jordan paused then nodded. "I can think of two women. One is of course your mother."

David inclined his head. "Thank you."

"The second is beautiful, sweet, loving and generous. I'd take her in an instant."

"Why don't you?"

"She's married to my brother. Makes the situation a bit awkward."

"There are other women out there. Your sister-in-law isn't the only one."

Jordan ignored him. "Unfortunately, Emma has one little flaw which would be the only reason I wouldn't take her."

"You just said you would marry her."

"No, I said I would *take* her. I didn't say I'd marry her."

David sighed. "What's her flaw? Besides the fact that she's in love with your brother?"

"She takes too much crap. At times I wish she'd tell my brother to take a pole and put it somewhere uncomfortable."

David laughed at the image. "She wouldn't dare."

"I know. I couldn't marry a woman I'd take advantage of."

"You'd take advantage of her?"

"I wouldn't mean to, but come on. When a woman does everything you want her to, wouldn't you?"

"No."

"You're lying."

David paused then nodded. "Yeah, I'm lying." He waved his fork. "So let me get this straight. You want a woman with her own business, who wants to start a family and who doesn't take your crap, but who you can control?"

"Yep."

"You're right. She doesn't exist."

"That's why I keep looking."

"Which takes me right back to my point. You can't commit to a woman. No one says you have to marry her, but dumping her—"

Jordan waved his fork.

"Having her dump you," David corrected. "Is not natural. You need to know why you do it."

"I don't care why."

"Your relationships with women are like an addiction."

"No, they're not."

David sat back and studied him for a moment. "I bet you couldn't go one month without a woman."

"Why would I want to? Life is full of choices."

David began to smile. "Four weeks."

"I like my life."

"One entire month. No sex and no new relationships."

Jordan began to rest his elbows on the table then recognized there was no room. He folded his arms. "Are you offering a challenge?"

David's smile grew. "You couldn't do it."

Jordan thought about Gail's tears. Perhaps he should take a break. He held out his hand ready for the challenge. "You're on. Just name your price."

Twenty-four hours later he met the woman who could cost him three thousand dollars.

Chapter 4

"What time is it?" Simone asked, stretching in her chair.

Dawn yawned. "I don't know." She glanced at the plastic dishes and utensils on her desk. Outside a street light flickered over the two lone cars in the parking lot. She didn't care how late it was. She planned to put together the perfect presentation package.

Simone hit a key on her laptop. "I still think the PowerPoint presentation is overdoing it a bit."

"Just check the slides. I don't want them too

crowded. Mr. Taylor needs to know how competent we are."

"It's three o'clock in the morning." Simone stood. "When is your appointment?"

"Around seven."

Simone spun Dawn around in her swivel chair. "You need to sleep. You don't want to go to the meeting with bags under your eyes."

"Don't worry." Dawn turned back to her desk. "Lately, I haven't needed much sleep."

"Dawn, you're a great consultant. You built one business, you'll build another. Now it's time to go home."

"But I need to assess the other schools…."

"No."

Dawn stared at her computer monitor. "We need this job."

"But he can't know that. You'll need to be cool and calm."

How could she be cool and calm? Dawn thought on the way home. This was her big chance, perhaps her only chance. A client like The Medical Institute could put her back on track. Soon she'd be able to afford a one-bedroom with a balcony, she'd be able to pay membership to a gym, and get her old life back. Taylor had no idea what this meant to her. He was probably at home sleeping without a care in the world.

The rich rarely had worries. She wondered what he was like. Was he handsome? He really didn't have to be; he had a great voice. She didn't know much about Jordan or the Taylors, but she did know that Charles Taylor had started the company. She had heard of a son named Ray, but never of Jordan. Why the change of successor?

She brushed the thought aside. Their family drama wasn't her concern. Her number one goal was to impress Jordan Taylor and get the job.

At home Dawn opened her closet. She didn't want to wear anything too severe or too casual. She had to project the right image. The more Taylor left to her the easier it would be. And the more credit she could claim. Her first goal was to get him to say "Yes."

A high shrill pierced through Jordan's peaceful slumber. He groaned and turned onto his side and pulled the covers over his head, but the ringing didn't stop.

He grabbed the phone. "Hello?"

"Hello, Jordan," a feminine voice said.

He liked the voice. Perhaps he was still dreaming. "Who is this?" He rubbed his eyes.

"It's Maxine."

His stomach twisted into knots; he became wide awake. He glanced at the clock: It read 4:30 a.m. "Do you know what time it is?"

"I knew I couldn't get you otherwise."

"This is not a good time."

"When is a good time?"

"A day after never," he grumbled then yawned.

"That's not fair," she said without anger. She kept her voice low. "Jordan, I need to see you."

He sat up and rested his head back. "Why?"

"I have to discuss something that I can't say over the phone. This is important to me and to you."

He turned on the light and squinted at the glare. "To me?"

"Yes."

His tone grew concerned. "Is someone ill?"

"I'll tell you when we meet."

He shut his eyes. "Maxine, you know I don't like games."

"Please, Jordan."

He didn't want to see her again. He still didn't trust himself. "I don't know."

"Please."

He held his head. "I shouldn't."

"But you will."

Damn, she knew him too well. "It will have to be quick. I have an appointment at seven tomorrow or rather today for dinner. You could come before then…say, around five."

"Fitting me in around appointments? Seems the tables have turned. Maybe you'll understand my position now."

"It won't change anything. We'll still be divorced."

She paused then said, "I hear you're the new head of the Institute. I wonder why Charles chose you."

"He wanted to make everybody laugh."

"If you need any business advice—"

"Right," he cut in ready to get back to sleep.

"I'll see you around five."

"Maxine," he said sinking under the covers. "This had better be good."

"Are you out of your mind?" Jordan stared at Maxine in disbelief. He surged to his feet. "No way!"

Maxine sat on the couch and tucked her feet under her. She kept her classically beautiful face composed and maintained a level tone as though dealing with a child throwing a tantrum. "Jordan, just listen."

He gestured to his ears. "I was listening. I can't believe what I just heard. Actually, I hope I didn't."

"You're being emotional."

"As opposed to psychotic?" He threw up his hands. "I don't believe this."

Maxine swung her feet to the ground. "It's a little favor."

"I'd rather extract my own kidney."

"I'm not asking for a kidney. I'm asking for a baby."

"That's nice. I hope you get one."

"I want to have it with you. Where are you going?" she demanded when Jordan abruptly left the room.

"To get something to eat."

She followed him to the kitchen. "I thought you said you had a dinner date."

"It's not a date. It's an appointment."

"I just saw you eat a sandwich."

"I'll still be able to eat dinner." He grabbed an apple.

Maxine stared at him amazed. "I always swore you had a second stomach. How could a man eat so much and still look like you?"

"Good genes." He waved his apple. "Which I'm not planning to share."

"You wanted to once," she said quietly.

"Then we should have had this conversation at that time."

"I wasn't ready then."

"And I'm not ready now. Go to a sperm bank."

Maxine hugged herself, her brown eyes pleading. "I want to know the father of my baby."

He stared at her for a moment then turned away. "No."

"Just think about it."

"No." He leaned against the fridge and kept his gaze on the ground. "The only way I'm going to have a baby is if I'm married to its mother, and since I don't plan to marry again, that won't happen." He raised his gaze, his tone unyielding. "Understand?"

Maxine shivered. "Don't look at me like that. That doesn't sound like you."

"Well, it is me."

"It didn't used to be. We both know how much you want kids. You can't deny it. I know you better than anyone. I know how much you wanted a family."

He smiled cruelly. "Yes, and we know how much you cared."

She blinked back tears. "I said I wasn't ready."

Jordan pushed himself from the fridge. "No,

you married the wrong son," he said in an ugly tone. "You should have married the one that was legitimate. That would have given you better business connections. The one that would have put you in the right circles."

Maxine widened her eyes, astonished by the accusation. "I didn't marry you because of who your father was."

He shrugged. "It didn't hurt being Mrs. Jordan Taylor. It got doors opened and helped with the popularity of your boutique. But running a successful boutique wasn't enough. You had to run me too."

"I wanted you to improve yourself. You had to do something with your life."

"I was doing something. I was living it."

"You were traveling and volunteering your time at that swim center."

"Why not? I liked it. I liked the hours and I liked the kids. I liked doing exactly what I wanted."

"Do you think being a CEO will give you time to do what you used to?"

"I'll make it suit me, not the other way around."

"Life isn't like that. You have to fit in."

"Why try? I'm worth more than your three boutiques combined."

"And you didn't earn a cent of it," she spat out.

He nodded, then said in a soft voice, "Yes, and you still resent that."

"I resent a man who could live for nothing else but pleasure when other people struggle."

"You resent me, yet you still want to have a child with me?"

"Yes. Because I know you'll make a great father."

Jordan winced as though she'd struck him then an unreadable look crossed his face. "No."

"You don't want to get married," she pressed. "But I know you want to be a father. It could work out for both of us."

"My parents weren't married. It might have suited them but it made my life hell. I won't subject my kid to that. I can't believe you're asking me to do that. Me of all people. I know what it's like to be part of a bargain. To be a piece in a game. My mother made my father pay for my existence. You're right, I didn't earn a cent of my money. I got a nice sum and made wise investments and I don't deserve any of it."

"I didn't say that."

"There are a lot of things you don't have to say."

"If you do this for me, I won't ask you for anything more."

Jordan tossed the apple away and grabbed a banana. "No."

Maxine sighed. "Stop fooling yourself. You'll marry again. You can't stand being alone." She placed the brochure on the table. "Think about it." She touched his cheek. He moved away. "Think about what you're saying no to. It may be your only chance."

Jordan rested his forehead against the door after she left. A baby. Damn, why now when she knew how much he'd wanted it then? How he'd wanted a wife and child and home life he'd never had. He shook his head. It was too late now. He didn't want anything to do with her or any woman. Not in that way. He wouldn't be that vulnerable again. He moved away from the door. The conversation never happened. The issue was over. No more women. Just business.

Over an hour later Jordan looked at his crooked tie in the mirror and scowled at his reflection. Why couldn't he get this right? It was such a simple task; men around the county, heck around the world, did it every day. Why was it so difficult for him? He undid it and tried again; then the doorbell rang.

He glanced at his watch and scowled. One thing he disliked more than ties were appointments that arrived twenty minutes early. He grabbed the two ends of his tie and answered the door.

"Hi, I'm Dawn Ajani."

Jordan stared as though he'd been punched in the gut. She was all wrong. She wasn't supposed to be that attractive. She had the proud dominant cheekbones of a West African heritage that made him think of desert winds, the heat of a blazing summer storm and the cooling rain that soon followed. She looked like a woman who could start a fire in a man and easily put it out. This was not good. He shook his head, feeling a little dizzy. Business. He had to think business.

And she looked ready for business dressed in a full gray pinstripe suit with a *tie*. Strangely, it made her figure appear more feminine.

"Nice tie," he said, then mentally kicked himself.

She smiled, he swallowed. She was even prettier when she smiled—bright, real, genuine. He shifted and coughed knowing he was staring.

"Thank you. I know it's not the trend, but I think the look suits me. Is it safe to assume you're Jordan Taylor?"

"Yes."

She held out her hand. "It's a pleasure to meet you."

He quickly shook her hand then took a step

back. He had to keep his distance. "Come in. Please take your shoes off." Along the foyer hallway, he had his shoes neatly placed in a row.

She slipped out of her shoes, left her briefcase by the door and headed to the living room. "I'm sorry I'm so early. I'd set my watch fast and forgot. However, I'd rather be early than tardy. Don't you agree?"

Jordan opened his mouth to reply, but she continued. "It's much better not to keep someone waiting. It shows good manners." She abruptly stopped and turned, Jordan crashed into her. They fell against the wall. He jumped back before he began to enjoy her softness beneath him.

"Sorry," she said.

He grunted.

"I just wanted to say that I see you're not completely ready so I'll just sit here until you are. Rushing people because you're early is equally as bad manners as being late. Don't let me keep you. I know how to entertain myself. And you don't have to worry, I won't snoop. I know how upsetting it is to have people who snoop."

Jordan stared at her.

She frowned. "Is something wrong?"

He flashed a look of mock surprise. "Oh, you mean I'm allowed to speak?"

Embarrassed, she cupped her face with both hands, looking up at him with a wide-eyed look. "I'm sorry, I didn't mean to go on like that. It's just sometimes I get on a topic and my mouth moves until the topic is finished."

"So—"

"Fortunately, I'm learning to listen more. I'm an excellent listener. In my field, it helps to make sure that my clients feel that their concerns are being addressed. I can assure you, Mr. Taylor, that you can feel confident that all your ideas, suggestions, concerns or whatever else will be heard."

"Ms.—"

"I can't tell you how excited I am by your proposal. I was able to flesh out many of your ideas. I think it's great that the Institute has selected a new president to give it a new direction. I believe that this endeavor is adventurous, though extremely ambitious, but…" She paused and drew her brows together concerned. "Mr. Taylor, if you're not careful you'll strangle yourself with that tie."

Jordan loosened his grip. "For a brief moment that had been my intention," he said gravely.

"Why?"

"I was hoping that if I passed out you would stop talking."

She covered her mouth then let her hand fall. "Again, I apologize. I—" He shot her a glance; she bit her lip. "I'll stop." She made a motion of zipping her lips closed.

"Good. May we get down to business?"

She nodded.

"Let me get my jacket." He disappeared before she could reply. He went into the bathroom and shut the door. He stared at his reflection and began to arrange his tie.

"She's not my type," he told himself. "I don't like women who talk too much and I don't like pushy women. She's both. That means I'm not attracted to her. I'm just excited about her ideas. I don't care that she's good-looking. That I'm thinking what she's like not suited up. I am not interested." He took a deep breath then left the bathroom. He saw Dawn on the ground putting things in a plastic bag.

"What are you doing?"

She glanced up. "Sorry, I knocked it over." She gestured to the hall table. "I wasn't snooping." She picked up a box of hair dye. "You have gray hair already?" she asked, surprised.

"No." He took the box from her and the plastic bag with other items he had purchased from the drugstore, the night before.

She stood. "Then why dye your hair? What color is it?"

"Doesn't matter."

"I'm curious."

He shrugged.

She gave him a flirtatious look. "There are ways of finding out."

"Well, that's one way you won't find out."

She lowered her gaze, embarrassed; Jordan fought a smile. "Right of course," she said.

He opened the closet and grabbed a coat. "The restaurant is a few blocks from here."

"Okay. I'll give you more time to get ready."

He closed the closet. "I am ready."

"Um, your tie is crooked. Would you like me to fix it?"

No. He didn't want her touching him. He yanked off his tie, tossed it on the hall table and opened the door. With that eloquent answer she followed him outside.

Chapter 5

He was a riddle set to music, Dawn thought as she sat in front of Taylor at the Little Tavern Greek restaurant. Jazz? No. There was no unrestraint or animation to him. Classical wouldn't suit either. There was too much soul burning beneath the surface. Country? He was certainly a transplant to the Washington Metropolitan area. He had a slow, thoughtful manner, a definite contrast to the fast pace of the city, and a hint of a carefully tempered southern drawl. But he wasn't that nor rock or R&B.

She couldn't pinpoint him. Dawn continued to

study him behind her menu; she'd been sneaking glances at him since they'd first met. Had he not been a man, she would have called him beautiful, but his contradictions got in the way of such a simple description. Everything looked dwarfed around him. The chair he was sitting in looked like a toy, yet he moved with grace. He had a thin top lip as though drawn by a ruler, but his bottom lip was full and sensuous. She wondered if that feature annoyed him.

His eyes were a surprise. When his gaze first fell on her face she'd taken an involuntary step back. She had expected dark-brown eyes, but his were light-brown. They looked the color of biscuits just pulled out of the oven. However, they didn't reveal much. Not warmth or coldness—nothing. She couldn't say the same for his voice. It betrayed a number of emotions in one word. That's when she knew how to describe him. He was an opera, bold, majestic, and enthralling.

She moved her gaze from his face to admire her surroundings. Large mirrors in gilded gold frames, hung on blue brocade wallpaper, reminiscent of an old Victorian mansion. Miniature votive candles were strategically placed next to the white china, and gold leaf cutlery was set on white linen tablecloths. In the middle of the table, fresh pink roses added a delightful fragrance. He had great taste in restaurants. Unfortunately, all she could think of at that moment was that the dinner was going to be a huge payment on her credit card.

"Are you ready to order?" Jordan asked.

Dawn returned her gaze to the menu. "I'm still looking."

"Take your time. Do you mind if I order?"

"No. Go right ahead."

He turned to the waiter and placed his order. Dawn listened with interest then disbelief as he ordered two appetizers, an entrée with three side dishes and dessert. "Bring it all at once," he said, closing the menu with a snap. He looked at Dawn and frowned. "Are you okay?"

"Yes, yes." She hastily glanced down at her menu. She didn't know what she was looking at. The only words that looked familiar were gyro and moussaka. She ran her hand down the selection of choices, pretending to know what she was doing. She didn't want to spend money on something she couldn't eat.

"Should I come back?" the waiter asked.

Dawn turned a page. "Umm…"

"I think you should get the pastitsio," Jordan said. "Do you like pasta?"

She looked at him relieved. "Yes, that's right. I'll have the pas...that." She handed the waiter the menu and watched him leave. "Thank you."

"You're welcome."

Dawn wrung the napkin in her lap. Now that they had placed their orders she didn't know what to say. She wanted to tease him about his large request, but he didn't look the type that took teasing well. Instead she looked at the tablecloth until she could see the fine stitching.

She had to concentrate. He was a potential client. She wouldn't think of him as a man. She looked up from the table and saw him glancing at a couple smiling at their baby.

"Do you know them?" she asked surprised by his intense look.

He shifted his gaze to her, and Dawn gripped her hands in her lap wondering when she'd get used to his piercing stare. "No. Why?"

She shrugged. "Just curious."

He glanced at the couple again. Dawn watched amazed as a cool red color washed over his face.

"Are you okay?"

"I'm fine. Thank you."

"You look a little flushed. If you need them to turn down the temperature I'm sure they would—"

His gaze stopped her. "I'm fine." He glanced at the couple again.

She swallowed her tea. "They have a cute baby."

His eyes met hers. "Yes," he said in a neutral tone. "Do you like children?"

She clumsily set her teacup down. "Yes."

"Planning on having any?"

"Not any time soon."

"You can't wait forever," he said with an ironic twist to his words. "You wouldn't want to suddenly get desperate."

"No."

He leaned back and watched her. "I'm sure that right now your career comes first. A husband and baby would get in the way."

Dawn frowned, unnerved by the bitterness she detected in his voice. "I assure you, that if the right man comes along he wouldn't be in my way and we'd raise the child together. Many couples do that."

"Yes, but nowadays most women don't need a husband, right? You can make your own money and rear your own kids. You just need the sperm and then you're on your way. Men are disposable."

She sipped her tea.

He stared at her for a moment until she squirmed in her seat. "No reply?" he said. "Aren't you going to defend your sex?"

"Why reply to someone who has already made up his mind?"

He looked at her, surprised, then embarrassed. "You're right. I apologize." He folded his arms. "So, who else have you worked with?"

"David Schelling."

"Who?"

"My dentist. His practice was failing until I helped him."

"I see."

"I also worked with the Tantland Pet Hotel. You can trust me to help you."

"I want to bring The Medical Institute up to current standards. Introduce the latest technologies, and set it apart. I want it to be known for excellence."

Dawn readied herself. This was the moment she had been waiting for. She was prepared. She moved her bread dish aside, and set her portfolio on the table and opened it. She handed Jordan a color brochure and business card. "With my help I can make that dream a reality. As a consultant, what I do first is to meet with you to discuss what you want done. During this initial meeting, I will evaluate and assess what you have currently, and what changes, and or modifications will need to be done, in order to achieve your intended goal.

"I will customize a comprehensive business

plan, that will include all my recommendations. For an additional fee, my services are available to help with the implementation of the recommendations. My business approach is basically simple. I select a team of advisors, each with experience in the areas we will be addressing. I will learn about current standards currently in operation for institutes such as yours.

"I will conduct on-site visits to assess and evaluate current practices in use, and look for innovative and unique ways to set the Institute apart. For example, the Institute is strategically located in an area where there are some excellent medical institutions. There's Johns Hopkins Hospital, the University of Maryland Medical Center and the National Institutes of Health. With increased visibility, and a stellar reputation, part of my plan would include recommending that the Institute develop ongoing relationships with these entities.

"Field trips could be scheduled to provide an opportunity for your students to visit these centers and see that they are part of a bigger picture, and for some of your graduates, they may be encouraged to further their education. I'm a firm believer in opening doors."

"Interesting. Tell me more." He clasped his hands together. "I'm listening."

Dawn talked until the food arrived. Jordan's order took up most of the table, but he frowned when he saw Dawn's fried fish flounder. "That is not what we ordered."

The server shook her head. "But on the slip it said—"

"I don't care what the slip said, that's not what we ordered." Dawn saw a faint hint of red begin to fill Jordan's face again. Not a good sign.

"I'm sorry," the server said, taking the plate. "We can take this back and start—"

"How long will that take?"

"I don't know, but I'll tell the chef it's important to hurry."

"That wasn't my question—"

Dawn touched his hand. "That's okay. I can eat this."

"Yes, you can, but you're not going to. Just take it away," he told the server. "She'll share my meal. Please get us an extra plate."

Dawn looked on, in shock, as the server hurriedly took her plate away. "Mr. Taylor, I could have—"

"They get their fish in on Monday. The best day to eat it though is Tuesday. Even so, they only do a tolerable job at best. They do everything else well, but the owner tries to foist as much fish as he can on unsuspecting customers because it's not a popular dish. It wasn't a mistake, it was a planned error. It's happened before."

The server reappeared with the extra plate. "Again we're sorry."

"Hmm." Jordan watched her leave. "I hate when they do that."

"It's okay." Dawn glanced down and noticed her hand was still covering his and hastily pulled away. "I've always found it's best to count to ten when I'm upset."

He looked at her surprised. "Who says I'm upset? Hand me your plate."

She did and watched him load it with zucchini sticks, miniature spinach pies, stuffed chicken breast, glazed lamb chops with baked garlic, and grilled spring vegetables. "Are you sure you'll have enough left over for yourself?" She teased, knowing there was still enough on the table to feed five people.

He didn't catch the joke. "I'll get something more later. Now let's get back to your ideas."

Two hours later all the food had disappeared and Dawn's voice was hoarse.

"You may meet with some opposition," Jordan said, looking at a slide on her laptop.

"That's fine," Dawn replied. "I will be as unobtrusive as a ghost."

"Somehow I doubt it," he muttered. He motioned to their waiter who immediately approached the table. "We're ready for our ticket."

Dawn picked up her purse. "Now how are we going to split this? I know that—"

Jordan gave her a light kick under the table and used her stunned silence to hand the waiter his credit card. The waiter bowed and left.

Jordan turned to her. "Relax."

"What?" she sputtered.

"You heard me."

"You kicked me," Dawn said amazed.

He raised a brow, the picture of innocence. "Now why would I do that?"

Before Dawn could reply, the waiter returned. Jordan signed the ticket then stood. "Let's go."

Moments later they walked back to his house. Dawn shot him a glance, wondering what to say, but he didn't seem prone to talk. He moved at a leisurely pace. However, he didn't have to move fast—his long legs ate up the distance. They finally stopped by her car.

"Thank you for your insight," he said.

"Yes, well—"

"I'll call you."

She grabbed his arm before he could turn. "This isn't a date, Mr. Taylor. I need to know if you would like to work with Ajani Consulting or should I spend my time on other projects?"

Jordan rested his hands on his hips and shook his head. "You're doing it all wrong."

"What?"

"You're going for the straight approach. That rarely works. In business you have to seduce potential clients." He suddenly frowned. "Scratch that. I mean *persuade* people. Don't act desperate. Act as though you don't need my business." He waved his hand before she could speak. "It's a suggestion, not a question. You don't need to reply. There are a few things I need to consider. I agree your time is important so I'll call you as soon as I can. Good night." He waited until she entered her car and started the engine, then he walked up the stairs, waved and closed the door.

Dawn stared at the door a moment then got out of her car and marched up the steps. She pounded on the door.

Jordan swung it open. "Did you forget something?"

She lifted her chin defiantly. "I don't need your business."

"Yes, you do." He softened his words with a wink then closed the door.

Dawn raised her hand to knock again, then let it fall. He knew she needed the work. She couldn't bluff him. So, he thought business was like a seduction? He didn't look easy to seduce though he'd probably been the seducer on a number of occasions. He was a mystery she planned to unravel.

When Dawn reached home, she was greeted by three messages. All from Simone asking how the meeting went. Dawn fell on the couch and stared up at the ceiling, then began to smile. Business as a seduction. Hmmm…that was interesting.

The next evening, Jordan decided he would hire her. He probably shouldn't, but he would. He had a day to think about it. The more work she did, the less work for him. He stared at the two-foot sub sandwich loaded with green peppers, lettuce, cheese and bacon bits. He took his knife and cut it in half and began to whistle. Today had been a good day. He'd avoided Maxine's three calls. He would win three thousand next month, and he was going to hire a consultant to help improve the Institute.

He hadn't been able to sleep last night, only

because he had a lot to think about, not because he was thinking about Dawn. He walked into the living room with his soda and sandwich and sat down.

Just as he lifted it for a bite, the phone rang. He glanced at the number, then his sandwich, then the number again. He chose the sandwich. At last the phone stopped ringing. A few minutes later it started again.

Jordan looked at the number then set his sandwich aside. "Hello?"

"We need to talk," Elena said.

"Nice to hear your voice," he said with false cheer. Hearing from his father's wife was never good. "How are you doing? Nice weather we're having."

"Cut the crap, Jordan. This is important. We need to talk."

He slumped lower in his chair and picked up his sandwich again. Elena would do most of the talking. "So talk." He took a bite.

"I hear that you've hired a consultant." When he didn't reply she said, "Did you hear me?"

He swallowed. "Yes."

"Are you eating while I'm talking to you?"

"No." He took a smaller bite. "Keep talking."

"You haven't answered my question."

"I didn't hear a question."

"You hired a consultant."

"Yes." Jordan paused, waiting for more. "What's your question?"

"I think it was obvious."

He rested his head back a moment and shut his eyes. "I'm a little dense. You have to help me out. Tell me what's wrong."

"You know what's wrong."

He reached for his drink, but his hand hit the glass at an odd angle and he spilled it. He swore.

"What did you say?" Elena demanded outraged.

"I wasn't talking to you, I spilled my drink. Elena. What. Is. The. Problem?"

"You hired a consultant!"

He grabbed paper towels. "Technically I haven't hired her yet."

She sniffed. "*Her*. It would be a female."

"What's that supposed to mean?"

"But you will," she continued. "All she has to do is smile at you and cross her legs."

"She won't have to cross her legs."

"Don't be disgusting."

He mopped up the spill. "I'm not. What are you thinking?"

She changed the subject. "Why do you need a

consultant? You know Charles only gave you this job to annoy Ray. When he gets better, he'll take over again. We both know Ray is the one who will inherit it."

"I don't care why he gave the position to me, I plan to make it work."

"It won't change anything."

"I think it will."

She hesitated. "Why do you need help anyway? The Medical Institute has run well for years. We don't need anyone coming in and changing things."

Jordan tossed the soggy paper towels away. "Minor improvements. I don't plan to do a major overhaul."

"People are nervous."

"Perhaps they should be."

"You may not realize this, but you have a reputation to uphold. As the president you have a lot of new responsibilities."

He poured another drink, feeling his patience thinning. "I know."

"Let Ray take over. You could be a figurehead."

"While he pulls my strings? Do I look like a dancing puppet?"

"You don't know how things are run."

He took a long swallow then set the glass down. "I'll learn."

She ignored him. "What is your plan? I mean, do you know what you're doing? The Institute is doing just fine. Did you go through the proper channels? Have you notified the board of what you plan to do? I'm on the board, and if you think you can just jump in and—"

Jordan hung up and unplugged the phone. "Yes, I can." He returned to the living room and sunk into the chair. He turned on the radio. An R&B song Gail used to play filled the room; he switched the station. A nice jazz song came through. He briefly wondered what Dawn would like then wondered what other less innocent things she would enjoy. He turned off the radio before his mind got too creative, then took a second bite of his sandwich.

Moments later, the doorbell rang. Jordan closed his eyes and swore. Would he have no peace? The doorbell rang again. "In a minute!" He quickly finished his sandwich, took a swig of his drink then put the dish in the sink. The doorbell rang again. "Dammit, I said wait." He raced to the door and opened it. "It would be you," he said to Ray. "I just got off the phone with your mother. What are you doing here?"

"I want to talk to you."

"You look upset. Are you drunk?"

"No."

Jordan patted him on the shoulder. "Then perhaps you should get drunk. You'll feel better." He stepped past him and pointed down the street. "There's a bar—"

"This isn't a joke." Ray pushed past him and headed for the living room.

"Take off your shoes."

Ray spun around. "What?"

"I don't like to vacuum so take off your shoes."

They stared at each other, then Ray removed his shoes and set them by the door. He walked into the living room and spotted a picture of his wife Emma and son Peter hanging on the wall. He looked away and took a seat on the couch. He jumped up when something hard bit into his thigh. "What the—?" He glanced down and picked up a pair of swimming goggles.

Jordan took them from him. "Great. I was looking for that pair."

Ray frowned then sat again.

Jordan fell sideways into a chair, his legs hanging over the side, and folded his arms. "Your mother didn't succeed and neither will you."

"You don't even know what I'm going to say."

Jordan nodded and threw out his hands. "True. Surprise me."

"How much do you need?"

His hands fell to his sides. "What?"

Ray leaned forward, resting his elbows on his knees. "Look, we both know that you took this position for the paycheck. You have a nice place and car, but it could always get better. I came up with an idea."

Jordan clasped his hands behind his head. "I'm listening."

"You let me run the show and I pay you a salary, then we slowly edge you out. You bow out gracefully and go back to what you do."

Jordan pretended to consider the idea. "No, thanks."

"You haven't thought about it."

"The answer is still no."

Ray gestured to Jordan's casual attire. "Look at you. You don't even have the persona of a CEO. You don't look like someone people can trust. A family man."

Jordan lifted a brow. "Like you?"

"Yes."

"Then you should be at home with your family, since you always like to throw it in my face."

"You leave them out of it."

"You do that pretty well yourself."

"This isn't about them, it's about us," Ray

said through clenched teeth. "Cancel with the consultant."

"Too late. I've already met with her. I'll probably hire her."

"It's not in our budget."

"We both know we can afford her."

"I can tell you all you need to know."

Jordan swung around to face his brother. "I'd like to trust you, Ray, but, unfortunately, I'm not that stupid. You might not believe this, but I want to make the Institute work. I plan to make it more technologically advanced."

"What do you think this is? College? These kids aren't smart enough."

"We can work with them."

Ray stood, shoving his hands in his pockets. "You don't know what you're getting into."

"I'll find out."

"You'll fall on your face."

"It's my face."

"And our name."

Jordan shrugged.

Ray's patience snapped. "I put twenty years of my life into this company."

"And I didn't have a chance to put in one," Jordan countered.

Ray shook his head. "What the hell are you

trying to prove? You think that being in charge will make you any more legitimate? You think that people will forget? You can't pass for one of us no matter what you do."

Jordan stood and walked to the door. "I'm pleased you came by today, little brother." He opened the door. "Say hello to Emma and Peter for me."

Ray pushed his feet into his shoes. "You're going to regret this. You're going to destroy what has taken us years to build and that will be your legacy. Everybody knows me and respects me. Don't fool yourself and think I'm the only one that looks down on you. Go ahead and hire a consultant, you'll be more of an outsider than you already are. It wouldn't be the first time that your presence caused unfortunate consequences." He stormed out.

Charles Taylor listened to his youngest son and silently laughed. "Yeah, yeah, I know about the consultant. Get some nerves boy, there's nothing to worry about. Yes, things are under control. Jordan can't do anything and this consultant will be gone before any harm can be done. Now go to bed." He hung up.

"What has you laughing?" his wife asked, sitting next to him in the grand living room usually reserved for guests.

"That boy of yours is real upset."

"He has every right. You shouldn't tease him about it."

"It's good for him. He needs some obstacles. People never know the value of something until it's gone. Besides, the way Jordan is going, he may not be president for long."

Elena smiled a little uneasily. "You're coming up with something?"

He didn't answer.

Her smile became brittle. She knew Charles was as clever as he was handsome. The minor heart attack had made him aware of his mortality, but hadn't decreased his vigor. He hadn't always been loyal, but she knew he wouldn't hurt his son. She touched his arm. He brought her closer and kissed her. "You smell good. Make the bed warm for me. I'll be right up."

"Okay."

Charles watched her go then stood and went to his office. Doctor's orders said he shouldn't be involved in anything too stressful, but he knew he couldn't leave everything up to chance. Jordan wasn't behaving the way he'd expected him to and Charles didn't like surprises. A consultant could mess up his system. He had to make sure she wouldn't uncover anything.

Chapter 6

"Do you think Daddy will like it?"

Emma Taylor looked down at her son Peter. He held up a picture he'd drawn using colored pencils. Shame he looked so much like his father, when they had nothing in common. He was already tall. People thought he was much older than his eight years. She looked at the carefully drawn picture of a building and swallowed a lump in her throat, fighting the coming of tears. *He won't even notice, honey*, she wanted to say, but didn't. Instead she patted him on the head. "Of course he will. It's beautiful."

Peter turned the picture towards him, doubtful. "He didn't like the last one."

"He was busy and wasn't paying attention."

"He's always busy," Peter said not out of bitterness but as a statement of fact. He was very practical, although she knew his father's neglect hurt him. "I'll show him first thing when he comes home."

"No, wait until dinnertime."

He looked at her, surprised. "You think he'll have dinner with us?"

"Lorraine will make his favorite."

"Oh, good. Maybe I can tell him about the City Project at my school. I'll go look for the flyer." He raced towards his room then slid to a stop. He slowly turned, his shoulders slumped. "Even if I did find it, he wouldn't come anyway, right?"

Emma forced a smile. "It never hurts to try."

"Yeah, it does," he said then walked slowly to his room.

Emma wished she could argue with him. Tell him that his father worked hard to support and take care of them. That he didn't mean to hurt them. That he didn't mean to make them feel as though they didn't matter. That had been the accepted excuse her mother used for her own father's long absences.

Determined to get his family up to the acceptable middle class, her father had worked two jobs. He had succeeded at the price of becoming a stranger to his wife and three kids. Many times she wondered if she had a father. She couldn't describe him for the first ten years of her life. At least her father's efforts meant something to them. He left treats on their bed, and she had wondered if her father was Santa Claus. But she knew that the sacrifice was for them. It had given her the opportunity to go to a good school and put her on the same path of the handsome and ambitious Ray Taylor. Meeting him had taken her far beyond her lower-middle-class roots to the fine three-acre estate she now called home.

At first she had been dazzled that a charismatic man, such as Ray, noticed her. Reality now showed that he hadn't really. He found her useful because she looked good beside him and knew how to run a household and organize a party. She knew his dedication to the Institute and his ambition to become president, came first in his life. He had plenty of money. He spent long hours away because he preferred the company of others to theirs and with each year things grew worse. Now Jordan was head of the Institute.

Emma glanced at the clock then went into the

kitchen to speak to the cook. She still had plenty of time to change the menu. She walked inside the kitchen and saw Lorraine chopping and preparing the evening meal. Lorraine had first worked for Ray's mother and father, and now for them the past three years. Her family had worked with the Taylors for generations. Joke was if you saw a Taylor a Macon was close behind.

Emma approached Lorraine, rubbing her sweaty hands together. She always felt like an outsider in the kitchen. Lorraine had claimed it as her domain and liked to needle her any time Emma messed up. "Could you please make grilled chicken with red potatoes?"

A large woman, made up mostly of muscle, not fat, Lorraine continued chopping without pause as though Emma hadn't spoken. She had an imposing, yet graceful figure with nimble fingers that created delectable dishes. She also had a way about her that made Emma feel useless. She knew if Ray had to make a choice he would choose Lorraine.

Emma cleared her throat. "Lorraine, I—"

"I heard you the first time. That was not on the menu you created."

"I know, I'm sorry." She hated that she felt the need to apologize. She had the right to change her mind. Lorraine worked for her, not the other way around. Emma rested her hands at her sides and lifted her chin a little. "I want to make Ray's favorite today."

Lorraine set the knife down and looked at her, her dark eyes assessing. "Is it a special occasion?"

"It doesn't have to be."

Lorraine smiled at her tense tone, a malicious gleam entered her eyes. "I'm only asking, Mrs. Taylor, because I would have to put the special dishes out."

Heat flooded her face; she glanced down, rubbing her hands together. "Yes, of course. That's very thoughtful." She looked up and shook her head. "No, that won't be necessary."

"Is there anything else?"

"No, thank you."

Lorraine rested her hands on the counter and flashed a knowing smirk. "You look very elegant."

"Thank you." Emma glanced down at the cream silk dress she'd purchased yesterday. The fitting had taken over an hour because she hadn't been able to keep still. She wanted everything to be perfect. An elegant dress that just might catch Ray's eye and let him know that there was more to life than work.

"Mr. Jordan has been the new CEO for two weeks now?" Lorraine asked. She masked the statement as an innocent question, both women knew it was not.

"Yes, I think so."

"Do you think Mr. Jordan will come by this week? I know his favorite dish, too."

Ray would never invite Jordan to dinner. Especially now. Lorraine knew this. "No, I don't." She hated Lorraine knowing so much about the family, although at times it seemed that she belonged in it more than Emma.

Lorraine had a history with them. Ray kissed her on the cheek more than he did his wife. She knew about the tension between the brothers. She knew Ray would not come home in a good mood and that the new dress and dinner were meant to appease him. She also knew the ploy was probably fruitless, and her malicious smirk soon turned to pity. "I'll start the chicken."

"Thank you." Emma left the kitchen and walked down the corridor. She could hear Lorraine chopping, this time with more vigor. Emma stopped in front of a family portrait, an oil painting Ray had commissioned. It showed them, in happier days, smiling. She had wanted the picture hung in the sitting room over the brick fireplace, but Ray had it put here instead. He put a large framed blueprint of the Institute there instead. Lorraine flustered her, because she knew and could see the truth of their marriage. Emma knew she knew she didn't belong there.

At times she hated the Institute. Why did Charles have to be such a cruel bastard? He knew how much Ray loved the company. He'd worked there since he was fifteen and everyone had expected him to become president one day, especially Ray. Charles's decision, selecting Jordan to take over, had been a bombshell. Jordan, who had never showed any interest in the Institute. Jordan, his illegitimate son who had been born to a woman Charles had slept with on a business trip.

She didn't know what he was up to, but she instinctively knew it wasn't good. Charles was never up to anything good. She'd known from the beginning what he was. She remembered their engagement party, Elena's cool grin and Charles's roaming eyes. She remembered that Jordan had been there, with one of his many lady friends by his side. He had shown and given approval.

"Are you sure you want to marry into this family?" he teased her.

"Watch out for him," Ray said. She thought he was joking, only to find out that Ray had meant it. But she knew Jordan wasn't what everyone thought. Neither was his father who'd smiled at her and given her a grand speech welcoming her into the family. Later that evening, Charles had taken her into his study and showed his approval of her in a way that still made her shiver.

She blocked out the memory. She'd promised herself she would forget that night. And she would.

She heard a car zoom up the drive and felt her heart accelerate like it had the first time Ray had driven up to her house to take her out. Even with all his disinterest, a look, a smile could still make her weak.

She went to the bar and poured a drink, then checked her hair in the hall mirror. She took a deep breath then hurried to the door and opened it before he placed his key in the lock.

Emma smiled when she saw him. "Hello, darling."

Ray didn't smile back. "Hi," he said, then placed a perfunctory kiss on her cheek and walked past. The cold April wind followed him, chilling her skin. Emma closed the door.

"How was your day?"

He hung up his jacket, closed the door and shot her a glance. "How do you think it was?"

"I don't know if you don't tell me." Not wanting to argue, she maintained her smile. She held up the drink. "Here."

He looked at the glass and shook his head. "No, I need something stronger."

"I'm sorry you had a hard day."

He glanced at her then marched down the hall. "Don't give me that." He went behind the bar and poured himself a drink. He took a long swallow, then smiled cruelly. "We both know how you feel about Jordan."

She set the glass down on the counter. "That's not fair, Ray."

"Well, life's not fair, right?" He finished his drink then set it down. He looked at her, his cold look softening a little. "I'm not singling you out. Everybody likes Jordan, except—" He stopped and poured another drink.

"Except you."

He lifted the glass as though offering a toast then swallowed its contents.

Emma sat on the stool and clasped her hands together gathering courage. "There's a way to make this work. Instead of letting it drive you further apart, perhaps you and Jordan can work together."

"Work together?"

"Yes."

"So, you expect me to help him and make him look good in a position that should have been mine? No, I'm going to watch him fall just like everybody else."

"He might not fall. What will you do if he makes the Institute more of a success?"

"It won't happen. He doesn't know how the Institute is run."

"You should be angry at Charles, not Jordan."

"It was just a test. Jordan wasn't supposed to accept. If he had any decency he would have bowed out, but he's a greedy bastard."

"Or maybe he wants to help. Charles is his father too."

"Only by accident."

"But—"

He sent her a dark look. Emma clasped her hands together in her lap. "Listen carefully," he said. "The Institute should be mine. It will be mine," he said in a low voice. "There is no question."

Emma spread her hands wide and swept one of them nervously across the counter until it touched his hand. "Lorraine is making grilled chicken with red potatoes."

Ray moved his hand away. "Good, she can

bring it to my office later." He came from behind the bar and headed towards the hall.

Emma absently touched the skirt of her new dress. "I thought we'd all eat together?"

He stopped and turned to her. "What for?"

"Peter drew a picture he'd like to show you."

"Another picture? The kid doesn't seem to do anything else."

"Please just tell him it's nice."

Ray shrugged, surprised by the request. "Sure. I'm used to lying."

"It's okay, Dad," a little voice said behind them. "You don't have to like it if you don't want to."

Ray spun around and for a moment a look of sadness and shame crossed his face. It soon disappeared replaced by cool nonchalance. "But I know I won't have to lie because you draw so well. Bring the picture."

"Mom said I was supposed to wait for dinner."

"I'll be busy at dinner. Go and get your picture now. I won't have time later."

Emma watched Peter leave then said, "Why can't we have a nice quiet dinner together?"

"We're not having this argument, Emma."

"I just want to understand why you can't even give us an hour of your time or even a half hour."

"Because I have things to do."

"Things won't change in an hour."

"Do you want to know what Jordan is up to?" he demanded in a harsh tone. "He's getting a consultant. Why the hell does the Institute need anyone's help? Jordan wants to invite outsiders to come and evaluate us. Do you know what that could do? No, you don't and neither does he. It's my job to stop him."

Peter came back and handed him the picture. "Here, Dad."

Ray glanced at it, then handed it back. "Hmm, looks familiar."

"It's the Lincoln Memorial."

Ray nodded and patted him on the back. "Nice. Good job."

Peter nodded, looked at his mother then back at him. "Um, at my school we're…we're…"

"Don't repeat yourself. It makes you sound hesitant. Just state what you mean."

"He's only eight," Emma said.

"Yes, a good age to learn to talk with authority. What were you going to say?"

Peter shifted awkwardly. "Um, ah…at my…at my school we're…" He lowered his gaze when his father frowned. "Uh, there's an event. I'm making a building."

"That's nice."

"I have a flyer."

"Another school event, hmm? Your mother will tell me all about it." He tapped the picture. "Good job."

Peter nodded, then turned and left.

"Thank you," Emma said with feeling.

Ray looked at his wife annoyed. "Don't sound so grateful. I wasn't lying. The kid has some ability. I just hope he grows out of this phase."

"His teacher at school thinks he's extremely gifted."

"Hmm." He shoved his hands in his pockets. "So you see my point, right? Jordan has to be stopped."

"I don't see the harm in getting another perspective."

Ray looked at her a moment. "No, you wouldn't. I don't know why I'm talking to you."

"I just—"

"I know. You want me to give Jordan the benefit of the doubt but that isn't going to happen. You're sweet and naive, but you don't know how business works." He turned towards the hall. "What are we having again?"

"Grilled chicken with red potatoes," she said softly.

"Good, I need that today. See you later." Emma watched him disappear upstairs then walked slowly to the kitchen. "Mr. Taylor would like dinner in his office." She turned before she saw the smirk on Lorraine's face.

Chapter 7

Jordan didn't usually hate the weekend, but this Saturday was hard. He had two days to think about his call to Dawn on Monday. Two days to think about what he would say and how she would respond. She'd be happy and he liked the idea of making her happy. She was good. He liked her ideas. She was smart and ambitious and he could control her...somewhat. She understood his vision. He was being objective. He wasn't hiring her for any other reason.

Although she talked too much and he occasionally thought about kissing her mouth closed, he wasn't hiring her because he liked her. He wasn't hiring her because he liked her enthusiasm and wondered if she did everything with such vigor. He was hiring her because it made good business sense. He'd worked with attractive women before. He could handle this.

After breakfast he sat in the living room, bored. What did people do by themselves? He could do this. He could be alone. He turned on the TV, and after watching endless commercials with couples, flipped it off and turned on the radio.

"Want to find your soul mate?" the announcer asked. "Don't be alone…." Jordan turned it off. Less than a week and he was already going crazy. He'd think about business, but when he thought about business he thought about Dawn and had very unbusinesslike thoughts. He changed into his swim trunks and went out through his kitchen and entered his enclosed pool and dived in hoping to clear his thoughts.

"Simone, stop checking the phone," Dawn said, just as anxious to see the office phone ring. She'd spent all weekend going over all that she had said at her meeting with Jordan and how she could have made it better.

"I'm just making sure the phone is working," Simone said setting the receiver down.

"Did we pay our bill?"

"Not yet."

"How many days left?"

"Two, I think." Simone crossed her fingers and closed her eyes. "But if Mr. Taylor calls—"

"Don't put any hope in that direction. I told you how our meeting went. He said he would think about it. It was a polite 'no.'"

"You gave him everything, didn't you?"

"I wanted him to know what we could do."

Simone threw up her hands. "How many times have I told you that you need to hold back a little? Now that you've given him an entire strategy, why does he need us?"

Dawn adjusted her skirt, uncomfortable. "I didn't give him that much. He'll still need to know which areas are in need of improvement and how best to incorporate these changes, without alienating current employees or losing any of his current students. Based on the information he shared with me, there's a lot that needs to be done."

Simone shook her head, exasperated. "This is how Brandon was able to use you."

"This is different. He's nothing like Brandon. Brandon I could influence. Taylor is as unmovable as a mountain with a body to match."

Impressed, Simone lifted a brow. "So you noticed?"

"It's hard not to," Dawn muttered. "Could you call the phone company?"

"They won't take any more excuses."

"If we pay that bill we'll be short on the lease." She rubbed her hands together. "I'll have to do some creative thinking."

"Call him and tell him you have more ideas. Perhaps that will interest him into offering you a contract. You have to have a little mystery."

"I'm not going to beg for work."

"I'll do it for you."

"No."

"We need to stay in business. This is a great opportunity. Do what you need to do."

The phone rang.

Simone answered it, then nodded. "One moment, please." She put the person on hold then did the sign of the cross and handed Dawn the phone. "It's him. Don't talk, just listen. This is our chance."

Dawn took a deep breath, then answered. "Hello?"

"I've gone over your package," Jordan said. "Very impressive."

Dawn struggled to focus, trying not to be dis-

tracted by his deep voice so close to her ear.
"Thank you."

"I'd like to work with you."

"I'll e-mail a contract to you right away."

"Could you bring it over instead? You could
stop by the Institute tomorrow morning. I'd like
to start right away. My calendar is free if you can
spare a few hours."

Don't talk, just listen. "Okay."

"Around eleven."

"Okay."

"Do you need directions?"

"No."

He hesitated. "Is something wrong? You seem
quiet."

"No, I'm fine." She grabbed a pen and started
doodling smiley faces. "I'm just jotting down
some notes."

"Okay. See you at eleven."

"Yes." She hung up.

Simone stared. "Well?"

Dawn ripped up the cutoff notice. "We're still
in business."

Dawn stood in front of The Medical Institute,
amazed that a place could look exactly like its
promotional brochure. It was an impressive two-

story, white stucco building that sat on four acres amidst carefully landscaped greenery. The sunny day encouraged one to explore the outdoors. She saw students sitting at various picnic tables, shaded by brightly colored parasols, eating their lunch. Others were gathered in groups, studying under trees, while others sat chatting around a large ornate fountain, decorated with sculptured figurines.

Dawn stepped inside, and tried to follow the directional map on the wall to orient her where to go first. She took the elevator to the second floor. The doors opened to a wide-open space, with high ceilings and skylights. Impressive green plants were strategically placed throughout, complemented by dark oak furniture. To the side of the elevator, Dawn saw what appeared to be a receptionist area. She approached the older woman sitting at the desk. The lady was draped in jewelry. Dawn could not help noticing five hoop earrings in one ear, and two in the other. Numerous gold bangles, on both arms, and at least five rings, made her appearance look like that of a fortune-teller, as opposed to a receptionist. Dawn approached her.

"I'm Dawn Ajani with Ajani Consultants. I'm here to see Mr. Taylor."

"Which one?"

Dawn hesitated. She'd forgotten he had a brother. "Jordan. I have an appointment."

The assistant pushed the intercom button. "Mr. Taylor, your appointment is here."

"Send her in," Jordan replied in a cool detached tone.

"He's in there." The assistant pointed to a door on Dawn's right.

"Thank you." Dawn approached the large wooden door and opened it. She saw Jordan sitting behind a large teak desk and smiled. He didn't smile back. Did he ever smile? She disregarded the thought and admired his surroundings. One day, with his help, she'd have an office like this. "I know I'm a little early. I had planned on being on the dot this time," she said. "Not too early or too late, but I had a bit of a hard time orientating myself. This building is enormous and the map on the directory downstairs wasn't very clear. We'll have to consider redoing it." The door closed and she noticed a man by the far wall. She suddenly felt the tension between them. He was as tall as Jordan, handsome but more conservatively dressed.

Jordan didn't rise from his desk, his cool gaze shifted to the man. "Ms. Ajani, this is my brother Ray. Ray this is the consultant I hired," he said with a strange emphasis on *hired*.

Dawn smiled, determined to ease the tension. She held out her hand. "A pleasure to meet you. From my understanding you worked closely with your father to make this a wonderful establishment."

Ray looked surprised, then pleased. "Thank you."

Jordan leaned back in his chair, watching them. "Ray needs a little convincing as to why we need your services."

Ray shot his brother a look then turned back to Dawn. "I just don't see why we need to tamper with a system that works."

"Probably because the system is out of date," Jordan said.

"If it ain't broke…"

"A record player can still play, but few people still use it."

Dawn spoke up. "I can understand your apprehension, Mr. Taylor, and I can assure you that we will take into consideration the integrity of The Medical Institute. My goal—I mean our goal—isn't to change something so much that it loses its uniqueness. I plan to work with you to do whatever is needed to bring this school into the twenty-first century. If you would like, I would love to meet with you another time. We can discuss some of your concerns."

"That won't be necessary," Jordan said.

Ray smiled. "I think that's a fine idea." He patted her on the arm. "It's been a pleasure to meet you."

"Here's my card," she said.

"I'll call you." He sent Jordan one last glance then left.

Jordan looked at Dawn. "Let's get down to business."

Dawn, aware that he wasn't in the mood for banal chitchat, opened her briefcase. "Here's the contract."

He read, signed the contract then stood. "Let me give you a tour."

"Don't worry about your brother. I think I'll be able to persuade him."

Jordan held the door open for her and gave her an odd look that sent a strange thrill up her spine. "Don't be too persuasive."

Confused, Dawn followed Jordan out of the office. An hour later, he turned down a main corridor, decorated with framed medical posters.

"My father started this school thirty years ago because he wanted to give low-income youth a chance at a good career," Jordan said, expanding on what he had discussed with her earlier. "Not everyone is meant for college and employment as a medical secretary, or medical or dental assistant pays well."

"I think it's wonderful."

"Thank you, but I want it to be much more."

"You have a lot of ideas. What did you do before this?"

"Nothing interesting," he said, inviting no room for comment. "So that's the end of the tour. Any questions?"

None that you'd answer. "Would you mind if I sat in on one of the classes?"

He shrugged. "Go ahead."

They returned to the receptionist area, and Jordan instructed the receptionist to show Dawn to one of the classes already in session. Then they parted. Jordan returned to his office and Dawn slipped into the back of a class, and sat on the cold hard surface of one of the classroom benches.

A pale skinny figure stood at the front of the class and moved with as much animation as the skeleton beside her. Dawn read the name on the desk. Mrs. Mortimer. Within five minutes Dawn felt her eyes drooping. Trying desperately to stay awake, she blinked and sat straighter. She glanced around the room. Most of the students had glazed looks. One student was fast asleep, drooling on the table. Dawn raised her hand.

Mrs. Mortimer paused as though amazed someone had a question. "Yes?"

"Excuse me," Dawn said in a clear voice that made everyone, even the drooling student, wake up. "Is this a course on handling emergency situations?"

She nodded. "Yes."

"Do you deal with real-life scenarios?"

"Yes, those are touched on."

"May I make a suggestion?"

Jordan sat on a windowsill, trying not to wonder what Dawn was up to, when Marlene buzzed him.

"Mr. Taylor?"

"Yes?"

"There's an emergency in Mrs. Mortimer's class."

He raced out of the room and down the stairs. He saw a crowd outside the door.

"I called the ambulance," a faculty member told him.

Jordan barely heard him as he pushed his way through the crowd. Inside the classroom people knelt beside a student who lay motionless next to a puddle of blood.

"What happened?" he demanded.

Mrs. Mortimer rushed up to him, her eyes

bright. She'd never looked more alive. "Patrick suffered a massive brain aneurism."

"What?"

"It must have been there for several years and had suddenly burst, causing him to have a major stroke. He's paralyzed on his right side. Isn't that wonderful?" She clapped her hands together. "Deidre is taking care of it right now." She pointed to a student taking vitals.

"This is a drill?"

"Of course. It was Ms. Ajani's idea."

"Yes, it would be," he said grimly. He turned to the crowd hovering by the door. "Someone please call and cancel the ambulance."

"Okay, that's enough," Dawn said. "Everyone back to your seats."

The fallen student jumped up and rushed to his seat. The others quickly followed.

"You did a great job," Dawn said. "Now I want everyone to write a paragraph or two about what just happened. How did you feel? How could things have been done differently? Don't worry, this won't be graded and it doesn't have to be Shakespeare."

"She's wonderful," Mrs. Mortimer gushed. "I'm so glad she visited my class."

Jordan folded his arms. "Hmm."

Dawn turned and hurried over to Jordan. "Did you see that?"

"Yes. I did." He did not look at her. Instead his gaze surveyed the group of students scribbling on their notepads. He noticed one of them constantly wiping her forehead.

"They really jumped into this activity."

Jordan nodded and watched the student more closely. Her skin looked pale. He glanced down when he felt tugging on his sleeve.

"Are you listening?" Dawn asked.

"No." He gestured to the student. "How long has she looked like that?"

"I don't know."

He searched his pockets. "Do you have some candy on you?"

Dawn searched in her pockets and pulled out a peppermint. "Here."

"Thank you." Jordan quickly walked over to the student and unwrapped the candy. "Have you eaten today?"

"I don't know," the young woman said, then slumped to the ground. Jordan barely caught her, preventing her hitting her head on the tiled floor.

"Great, another drill!" a student cried.

"This is not a drill," Jordan said. He lifted the woman's wrist, revealing an emergency bracelet.

"She's a diabetic. She looks like she's going into a diabetic shock." He patted both sides of her face, succeeding in her regaining some consciousness. "Come on, take this." He put the peppermint in her mouth, but it fell out. "Does someone have juice or soda?"

The previous "victim" rushed over with a bottle of grape juice.

"Come on," Jordan urged, pressing the drink to her lips. She was able to swallow some. Within minutes they heard the loud wail of a siren. Jordan sighed, relieved that they hadn't been cancelled in time. Moments later two EMTs entered the room and took over the situation.

Once the excitement had died down, Jordan turned to Dawn and indicated that he wanted to talk to her.

She walked up to him. "Yes?"

"I want you in my office in five minutes." He raised his forefinger when she opened her mouth. "Say a word and I'll make it two." He turned and left the room.

Chapter 8

"As unobtrusive as a ghost, you said."

Dawn swung her legs around, and adjusted her skirt, as she stared at Jordan across his desk. "I don't know why you're upset."

"You disrupted the entire class! No, excuse me. The entire school!"

"I had to do something," she argued. "They were falling asleep and unless they learn by osmosis, no amount of learning was going on. I had to liven things up."

"By frightening everyone?"

"I didn't frighten anyone."

"Someone called an ambulance."

She squirmed uncomfortably. "Yes, I hadn't planned on that, but it did come in handy." She paused. "You know you probably saved that girl's life. Where did you learn to detect negative insulin reactions?"

"I used to work with a lot of kids, and I took first aid."

"That was impressive."

He brushed the praise aside. "Now about the drill." He clasped his hands together and a pained expression crossed his face. "Was the tomato paste really necessary?"

"It made everything more dramatic."

"They don't need dramatic. They simply need to learn what is necessary for their positions. It's likely that most, if not all of these students won't be working in high-octane situations."

"You never know. You saw what happened. Your training helped save that girl. They could face a similar situation and would need to respond as coolly and calmly as you did. Just because they are training to be technicians doesn't mean they deserve to be bored to death."

"True. But the Institute is already known for its thorough teaching approach. We have, and continue to be, successful."

Dawn clapped her hands together. "I just had a great idea. This exercise could be an ideal way to give pop quizzes."

"The teaching methods, currently being used by the Institute's instructors, have been known for years," Jordan continued.

"Could you imagine if the students entered the classroom faced with a scenario they needed to solve?"

"We wouldn't want to change—"

"They could be given a list of instructions and a time frame in which to perform. Every class could use this method. We—"

Jordan pounded the desk. "Dawn!"

She jumped and stared at him. "Yes?"

"I want you to stay out of the classrooms."

"But I have suggestions that—"

"If you have any more suggestions," he said with exaggerated patience, "you can write them in your report which you will give to me."

"Okay." She jumped to her feet. "But there's something I have to show you."

"What?"

"It's in one of the classrooms. Don't worry, it's empty right now."

Jordan gave a weary sigh, stood and followed her with dreaded anticipation.

* * *

They entered a classroom at the far end of the corridor. Dawn turned on the lights. "Do you see this room?"

"Yes."

"It doesn't have an effective layout. It's not conducive to positive energy needed for optimal learning. It needs to be rearranged. Now watch this." Dawn whizzed back and forth across the room moving desks and chairs. She stopped briefly when she noticed Jordan holding his forehead.

"Do you have a headache?" she asked him.

"Probably."

"I could get you some aspirin."

He let his hand fall. "That won't make it go away."

"Oh." She grabbed a mannequin and dragged it across the room.

Before Dawn could move a large wooden bookcase, at the back of the classroom, Jordan jumped in front of her, startling her. "You talk too much and you move too fast. If you don't slow down you're going to hurt yourself. Now tell me what you want done."

For the next twenty minutes or so, they moved furniture. Moments later, Dawn rested her hands on her hips and looked around, satisfied. "What do you think?"

Jordan folded his arms, impressed by the changes. "It looks, umm...good."

"I can do this to the other rooms."

"No, that's not the way things are done around here. Provide me with a layout of how you would like each classroom to look. Please promise me that you will visit the classrooms only when there are no students present. I will take your recommendations, and if I agree with them, I'll instruct our building supervisor to do it for you. I didn't hire you to move furniture."

Not wanting to overstay her welcome, Dawn glanced at her watch. "Well, time to go. It's been a wonderful day. I can't wait to put my—I mean our—other ideas to work. I'll see you next week and I'll avoid the classrooms, I promise."

"I want you first."

Her mouth fell open.

"In my office," he corrected. "I mean I want you to come by my office first."

After parting with Dawn, Jordan took the stairs and spotted Ray. He considered taking the elevator, but Ray saw him.

"I heard about Mrs. Mortimer's class," Ray said. "Nice 'minor' changes."

Jordan didn't reply.

"Seems Ms. Ajani is already causing trouble. You'd better get a hold of her."

"That's the problem," Jordan said heading to his office. "I want to very much." He closed the door.

Ray shook his head at the odd statement then went into his office. He watched Dawn walk to her car from his office window. Her vitality struck him even from this distance. He picked up his phone and dialed. "I met the consultant," he said once his father picked up.

"What is she like?" Charles asked.

"Trouble. She could be dangerous if we don't watch her."

"Then we'll watch her closely."

"Jordan likes her."

"Jordan likes anything female."

"This one is different."

"How different?"

Ray watched her drive away then turned from the window. "I don't know. There's something about her."

"I don't like ambiguity. You find out what. Have you spoken to—"

"Not yet," Ray said quickly.

"It's not wise to keep him waiting. He'll still want the same arrangement we've established."

"But it's going to be tricky with Dawn looking into things. Maybe I should tell Jordan…"

"You leave Jordan out of this," Charles snapped. "Let him stay in the dark."

Ray gripped the phone. "If you didn't want him to know anything, why did you give him the position?"

"That's my business, not yours."

"It is my business when I have to clean up the mess he'll probably make."

"I thought I'd give you the chance to prove yourself. Do you want to quit?" Charles taunted.

Ray fell into his chair.

"That's what I thought. However, if you don't think you can handle her…"

"I can. I'm meeting with her for lunch."

"Good."

"I'll see what her plans are. She's very persuasive and we know Jordan's weakness for a pretty face."

"He's not that weak," Charles warned. "Don't underestimate him."

"I've taken care of Jordan, Dad. Don't underestimate me."

Charles chuckled. "That's what I like to hear. Goodbye."

Ray hung up the phone then went into the receptionist area. "I'll be gone a few hours," he told Marlene.

She glanced up from sorting the papers on her desk. "Your mail is here. Would you like me to leave it on your desk?"

He walked over to her. "No, I can look at it now." He took the mail from her, then noticed a large envelope addressed to Jordan.

"It's another notice from ACCTS," Marlene said, following his gaze.

Ray picked it up. "Interesting, I'd better look it over."

Marlene hesitated. "I think Mr. Taylor should see it first. It might be something important."

"Don't worry, if it's important I'll let him know," he said, tucking the envelope under his arm. He flashed a smile of reassurance. "Marlene, you know you can trust me. I'll make sure he gets it, just like I did last time."

Jordan sat staring at the blank TV screen. Another evening and he didn't know what to do with himself. He picked up the phone then set it down. There was no one to call.

He thought about Dawn and how she had redecorated the classroom. He had to admit, the changes she made, had greatly improved it.

Inspired, he rearranged his living room. By the next day he'd rearranged it back. The change reminded him of Dawn and Dawn reminded him that he couldn't have her in the way he wanted to, at least not right now.

He didn't know why he wanted her. She had all of the same characteristics that had broken up his marriage. A woman who was all business and wanted to do everything herself. A woman who didn't want to depend on anyone. No, he was not going to go through the Maxine thing again no matter how tempting. This bet was good. He needed this kind of space to think. He didn't need a woman in his life. There was no one to tell him what was wrong with him.

Jordan nodded, pleased with his conclusion, but he still felt restless inside. Sitting in his overstuffed lounge chair, he looked out the window and saw a man walking a dog. Suddenly, an idea hit him.

An hour later, Jordan stood in the reception area of the Dulane Humane Society.

"I'm looking for a dog," he said to the freckle-faced blonde at the desk. "Preferably large and short-haired."

The attendant turned her head and pointed to the metal doors, her large hoop earrings hitting her cheek. "Through there."

"Thank you." Once he passed through the doors, he found himself inside a large room filled with cages. Another attendant, with a row of tattoos on both arms, pointed him the direction of cages.

"The dogs we have available are over there," he said.

The sound of barking and paws hitting metal echoed down the row of metal cages. He would get a large breed dog, short-haired, perhaps a puppy he could train. He didn't want one with a set personality and bad habits. Lucky for him, he knew that Dulane was a no-kill shelter, so he didn't have the added pressure of worrying about seeing a dog on death row.

"Can I help you?" a young woman with two long braids asked in a voice as perky as the puppies in the cage next to her.

"I'm just looking."

"At the end of the row are more puppies and young dogs. Let me know if you need help."

"Thanks." Jordan headed down the row and saw a medium-sized black Doberman sitting regally. He stopped in front of the cage. "You're just what I had in mind." He was about to call the attendant when his gaze wandered to the next cage. At first it appeared empty then Jordan looked down—way down—and towards the back of the cage saw a little dog. It wasn't a puppy or one of those cute toy breeds one sees with the rich or royalty.

It didn't looked like any breed at all. It looked like a beagle and dachshund mix. The dog sat still on the cool concrete and stared up at him, its tail slowly moving side to side like a windshield wiper on the lowest register. It gazed up at Jordan through one green eye and one brown eye. Its gloomy expression seemed to light up when it saw him.

Jordan shook his head. "No." He returned his gaze to the Doberman, but felt the canine gaze like a tap on his shoulder. He moved away and walked farther down the row. He glanced back and saw the dog's paws resting against the cage.

Jordan walked back to the cage and squatted in front of it. The dog sat on its hind legs and again began wagging its tail from side to side. This time the rhythm was up a notch. "Look," Jordan said in a low voice. "Someone is going to come in here and like you. You've got shelter and food here. You're okay." He glanced around then back at the dog. "Yes, I know the bars are depressing, but you won't be here forever. I'm looking for a real dog. Something that actually looks like it has legs." He surveyed the sausage-like body. "That obviously isn't you."

The dog continued to wag its tail at an even faster pace.

The attendant came up to him smiling and said in a high chirpy voice, "Are you interested in Fruity?"

"No, I'm not interested in Fruity," he snapped. The woman stepped back, startled. Jordan softened his tone and stood. "I'm looking for something bigger. Thank you."

"Oh well, she's a good dog. We named her Fruity because she looks like a mixture of things. Like fruit punch."

"Okay." He moved away, not wanting to be pressured into taking the dog out of pity, and continued walking down the row. Most of the dogs were eager to get his attention. A few slept curled up in their cages, while others paced back and forth. Others climbed all over their cages, barking uncontrollably, trying to get him to stop.

Maybe he wouldn't get a dog. It would probably be too much work and he hated to vacuum. As he turned to go, he heard the metal doors slam and several pairs of sneakers squeak against the concrete. A little boy about his nephew's age rushed in. He ran up to Fruity's cage and cried, "Eww! Mom, Randi, look at that ugly dog." He pointed at the dog, and they all began to laugh.

"I don't care," Jordan muttered, feeling his temper rise.

"It does look strange. I don't want it," the boy said, poking Fruity with his finger.

"That's not nice," his mother scolded.

"Why are its eyes different colors? It's really weird."

The little girl, standing to the side of the boy said, "It's not so weird. I could dress it up and make it look pretty."

Fruity looked up at him with a "help me" look in her gaze. Jordan sighed. "Damn."

Jordan placed the dog on the passenger seat. "First thing is a name change. I'm not calling you Fruity. I saved you from being dressed up in tutus for the rest of your lift. So you owe me. I have a nice place, so try to be clean."

Fruity wagged her tail, then rested her paws on the window ledge looking at the passing scenery. "You're not listening. That's fine because I don't feel like talking."

Moments later, Lana came out of her front door and saw Jordan carrying Fruity out of his car.

"Are you dog-sitting?" she asked, watching him set the dog down.

"No." He looked down at the dog. "No, she's mine." He gently lifted Fruity's paw and said, "Meet your new neighbor."

"You got a dog?" she asked surprised. "That doesn't seem like you."

No, but because I couldn't get a woman, I decided to get a dog instead. "Yes," he said. "I thought it would be a nice change."

She came closer. "What breed is it?"

"A mutt."

Lana bent down and patted the dog on the head. "She's sweet. What's her name?"

"I'm not sure yet."

"She sort of has a reddish coat. You could call her Carrots." She winked. "Like her owner."

Jordan felt his face grow warm. "Thanks for the suggestion, but I'm sure I'll come up with something more suitable."

He walked up his front steps and saw a plastic bag leaning against his door. He picked it up and pulled out a book with a pink sticky note attached to the front. *Jordan, think about it. Maxine.* Think about what? he thought, removing the note. He saw a pink-and-blue rattle on a white background then the book's title: *1000 Baby Names.*

He looked down and waved the book at Fruity. "She could have been your mother." Disgusted, he tossed the book back in the bag and went inside.

He unlatched Fruity's leash and she immediately began sniffing her new surroundings. "Now you're old enough to tell me when you have to go. Come on, I'm going for a swim."

Fruity dutifully followed Jordan through the kitchen into the pool area. Jordan put on music then did a couple of laps in the pool while Fruity put her head down and watched. When he emerged from the water he heard the melodious voice of Dame Kiri Te Kanawa singing. Jordan grabbed a towel and sat on the edge of the pool. He looked at the dog. "That's what I'm going to call you. Kiri." The dog licked his face in approval and Jordan scooped her up and went upstairs.

By late evening they had settled into the couch and enjoyed an action movie. The doorbell rang. Jordan swore and looked at Kiri who had fallen asleep. "I'll teach you to attack one day." Her ears twitched.

The doorbell rang again.

"Hold on," Jordan said then answered.

"Hi," David said. "I came by to make sure a woman didn't answer."

"I told you I'm going to win."

David took off his shoes and walked into the living room. He halted, confused. "Your living room looks a little different."

"I made some changes then decided to switch it back."

David smiled. "Being alone is killing you, isn't it?"

"I'm fine."

He glanced around and saw Kiri sitting on the couch. His eyes widened. "What is that?"

"That's Kiri."

"Kiwi?"

"Kiri." Jordan tapped his thigh and called to the dog. "Come here, Kiri." She jumped from the couch and waddled over.

David looked down at her. "Is that supposed to be a dog?"

"I'm not sure."

David knelt in front of her. He held out his hand and she gave him her paw. He nodded, impressed. "She knows how to shake." He scratched her behind the ears and she rested her head against his thigh. "She's kind of cute in a weird sort of way." He shook his head. "I knew you couldn't do without female companionship."

"Feminists would string you up for that comparison."

"You have three weeks left."

"I'm going to win."

"You met that consultant the other day, how did it go?"

"It went well. She gave me that." He pointed to the stack of papers on his side table.

David whistled. "Very thorough." He raised a brow. "What is she like?"

"She's not my type. Very career-oriented."

"Like Maxine."

"Exactly."

"Maybe you can loosen her up," David said, then snapped his fingers in regret. "Nope, you can't. Not for three more weeks. You'll just have to imagine it."

"I'm not interested. I do like the way she thinks." *And moves and smells.* "It's only business. She has good ideas."

David picked up the stack of papers and flipped through them. "I can see." He set the folder down and saw a brochure on the dinning table with a strange drawing on it. He walked closer to get a better look. "What's that?"

Jordan followed him. "Oh, uh, Maxine came by."

"Why?"

"She needed to talk."

"About what?"

"None of your business."

Both men stared at each other then lunged for the brochure. David got to it first. He read the front. "Fertility?" He opened the brochure and raised his eyebrows.

"It's nothing," Jordan said.

David opened the brochure to its full length then held out an illustration of a woman's reproductive system. "That doesn't look like nothing."

"She wants to have a baby."

"With you?"

Jordan snatched the brochure and crumpled it up. "I told her it was a bad idea."

"Why keep the brochure?"

"I forgot I had it."

"Even if you wanted to…"

"Which I don't."

"You'd have to wait anyway."

Jordan threw the brochure away. "I'm going to win. I've handled Maxine, Gail is gone and Dawn—Ms. Ajani is purely business."

David smiled and glanced at the folder. "For now."

Chapter 9

The next week Dawn arrived early at the Institute and went directly to Jordan's office.

"Mr. Taylor isn't in yet," Marlene told her.

She glanced at her watch. "But it's eight-thirty. I thought the school starts then."

"Yes, but Mr. Taylor doesn't arrive in his office until ten-thirty."

"Oh."

Marlene stood to go to a file and Dawn noticed her anklet. "That is gorgeous."

"I know." She grinned. "My boyfriend bought it for me on a trip to New Mexico."

"I've never been."

"We're traveling there in three months. I could get you something."

"I doubt I could wear jewelry as elegantly as you do." Dawn glanced at her watch again. "What am I supposed to do? I can't wait for two hours."

"His brother Ray is here if you need to talk to someone."

"No, no, that's okay. I wanted to tell Mr. Taylor about my little experiment. I guess I'll see him later. I'm off to visit the dental instructors."

Jordan had a sinking feeling something wasn't right when he pulled into the parking lot and saw Dawn's car. She'd arrived before him. He'd forgotten she was always early. That wasn't good. He didn't picture her patiently waiting for him to arrive. He walked into the building and stopped at the sight of students wearing different colored lab coats. Some green, some red, some purple.

"What is going on?" he asked one of the students, a young man in a red lab coat.

"It's an experiment."

"What kind of experiment?"

"Color coded ranking. Beginners are green,

intermediate purple and advanced are red. The coats were handed out this morning at recruitment."

"I see. Thank you." Jordan walked past, sensing that the rest of the day probably would not go well.

Ray met him on the stairs. "What the hell is going on?"

"You mean I'm not hallucinating? That's a relief."

"This is serious."

Jordan winced. "There is no need to shout."

"Do you have a hangover?"

"No." He'd made the mistake of allowing his mind to wonder about Dawn. After nearly a hundred laps, two cold showers and three hours sleep, he felt exhausted.

"I thought you said minor changes," Ray said following Jordan up the stairs.

"They are wearing different-colored coats. That is not a major overhaul." A student passed them wearing pink polka dots.

"How do you explain that?"

Jordan cleared his throat. "I'll talk to her."

"Keep her in line, Jordan."

Jordan stopped and spun around. "I think the line you'd better watch is your own. I'm handling this." He walked to his office and greeted Marlene.

She held out an envelope. "This came for you."

"Thanks." He opened the envelope then frowned. It was a listing of the technical schools and the Institute had one of the lowest graduation rates.

"Is something wrong?"

Everything. "No. Thanks." Once in his office, Jordan sat behind his desk and stared up at the ceiling. He had to get Dawn under control. He looked over the listing again. And he had to raise the graduation rate somehow.

Nearly an hour later, Marlene buzzed him. "Yes?"

"You have visitors. Emma and Peter."

He relaxed. "Send them in."

Dawn read over her notes from her meeting with the three recruitment personnel with growing concern. It seemed that a lot of funding went into that program although the graduation rate was low. She flipped over her yellow pad then glanced at her watch: twelve forty-five. She was supposed to meet with Jordan at ten-thirty. She rushed down the corridor then took the elevator to his office.

"Is he here?" she asked Marlene.

"Yes. He has visitors, but I'm sure he'll want to see you. Just go right in."

Dawn entered the office and saw Jordan talking to a thin, conservatively dressed woman. Out of the corner of her eye she saw a little boy bent over a side table.

"This is my sister-in-law Emma," Jordan said. "And my nephew Peter. This is my—our—consultant, Dawn Ajani."

"Hello," Emma said. Peter waved then turned away.

"He doesn't talk much," Jordan said.

Dawn nodded. "Nice to meet you both."

"We'll be done in a minute."

"Okay." Dawn walked over to Peter and noticed his drawing. "Is that the Institute?"

He nodded.

She leaned closer, amazed. "That is outstanding. Did you trace from a picture?"

He shook his head.

"Do you mind if I look?" He pushed the drawing towards her. She studied it. "Hmm, now I don't remember seeing that wing." She tapped the picture.

He smiled. "That's 'cause it doesn't exist yet."

"You added it on?"

"Yeah, when I own the Institute I'm going to add a new wing."

"For what?"

He shrugged. "Don't know."

She patted him on the shoulder. "That's okay. You don't have to. It could be whatever you want it to be."

He stared up at her, curious. "I always add something to my drawings. You're the first person to ever notice."

"I'm sure others have noticed, but didn't question you about it."

"Maybe," he said doubtfully.

"So you take a building and make it your own?"

"Yeah. I added five extra pillars and another entrance to the Lincoln Memorial."

"Why?"

"I thought it would be nice."

"I would love to see your other work. I love looking at buildings."

His face lit up. "Really? What's your favorite?"

"I love Union Station and Grand Central Station."

"I've drawn them both. I can show you. At my school we made a city. I designed the mayor's building. It's in a few weeks. Want to come?"

"I'm sure Ms. Ajani has a busy schedule," Jordan cut in, his voice like an ominous storm across the room.

Dawn and Peter jumped, startled. They'd forgotten they weren't alone. "No, I won't be too busy," Dawn said. "I'd love to come."

Peter nodded, pleased. "Good. Uncle Jordan's coming so he can take you."

She glanced at Jordan and knew that was a poor suggestion. "That's okay. I can find my own way."

"Well, we'd better go," Emma said standing. "Let's see if your father has come back yet." She looked at Dawn. "Nice to meet you."

Peter handed Dawn his picture. "You can keep it," he said with a shy smile. "I have lots at home."

"Thank you. I can't wait to see the others."

He waved then followed his mother out the door.

"I've never seen him talk so much," Jordan said, amazed. He came up behind Dawn and looked down at the drawing. He read the inscription: *"To Don from Peter."* He shook his head. "You'll have to tell him how to spell your name."

Dawn stiffened from the scent of his cologne and closeness, hoping she wouldn't accidentally touch him. "He's delightful," she said carefully placing the picture in her briefcase.

Jordan frowned. "Do you think it's going to be worth something?"

"It's worth a lot to me. I'm going to frame it."

"You think it's that good?"

"Don't you?"

He shrugged. "It's nice. The kid draws all the time. It won't take him far."

"You'll be surprised."

He moved away. "Don't worry, I'll make excuses for you."

Her heart began to beat normally again. "What do you mean?"

"That school function he mentioned. You didn't have to accept the invitation to impress me. I know you didn't want to hurt his feelings."

"I said yes because I want to go."

"But something else might come up."

"You expect me to cancel?"

"Things come up."

She snapped the briefcase closed. "I'll be there."

"He'll be looking for you. I know him and he'll be hurt if you don't show up. He doesn't need someone else disappointing him."

"I'll be there."

"Is that a promise?"

"Yes, Uncle Jordan," she said in a singsongy voice. "I promise."

Jordan relaxed then returned to his desk. "Good." He sat. "Now about the lab coats."

Dawn sat also and eagerly leaned forward. "Don't they look great!"

He picked up a pen and muttered, "That wasn't the word I would use."

She pulled her chair up to his desk and rested her arms. "At first I thought the colors may be a bit loud, but bright colors affect mood in a good way."

"And can be distracting."

"I could tone them down a bit."

He tapped his desk with his pen. "Or go back to white."

Her enthusiasm dimmed. "You don't like the idea?"

"It's—"

"Because I can adjust the red to mauve. I purchased the jackets at a great discount and it was just an experiment. I, in no way, thought it had to be a permanent change." She made a wide gesture with her hand and knocked over his container of paper clips. They spilled into Jordan's lap and onto the floor. "Oh, sorry."

Jordan began to scoop them up. "It's okay."

Dawn came around the desk, fell on her knees and helped him.

Jordan looked down at her. "I can get them."

"It's no problem." She released a handful of paper clips into the container.

The door swung open and Marlene entered. "Mr. Taylor, I need—"

Dawn straightened and peeked her head from behind the desk. Marlene glanced at Jordan in the chair and Dawn on the floor and took a hasty step back. "Excuse me."

"Marlene, wait," Jordan said, but she'd already closed the door.

Dawn returned to picking up the paper clips. "I don't know why she looked at us like that." Then she stopped and glanced up only to discover that her eyes were lined up perfectly with Jordan's lap. She looked at him stunned.

Jordan saw the look on her face and burst into laughter.

"It's not funny." Dawn jumped to her feet. "I have to explain."

Jordan grabbed her wrist. "We both will." He hit the intercom. "Marlene, please come in here."

"Yes, Mr. Taylor."

Dawn tried to free her wrist. "I should go to her."

"You're staying right here," Jordan said, pulling her back. She lost her balance and ended up on his lap just as Marlene opened the door. Her mouth fell open.

Dawn leaped to her feet. "It's not what you think. I wanted to explain it before, but Mr. Taylor grabbed my wrist and I wanted him to let go, but he wouldn't so I pulled one way and he pulled another and I tripped and fell back. And ow!" She cried when Jordan pinched her.

"What Ms. Ajani is trying to say, so succinctly, is that what you saw was a misunderstanding. It was perfectly innocent."

"Yes, I thought so," Marlene said looking relieved. "Excuse me." She left the room.

Dawn returned to her seat. "Whew. That was easy," she said, pleased. Then she became annoyed. Why had Marlene been so quick to believe them?

"Now back to the lab coats." He held up his hand before Dawn could argue. "You're not to make any other changes without consulting me first. No exceptions. Based on the proposal you presented to me, we agreed on the following." Jordan picked up a navy blue binder on his desk and opened it. "Number one, replace equipment in teaching lab with more up-to-date versions. Number two, install new cooler system for storage area to better adjust temperature for lab specimens. Number three, purchase newly designed teaching models to replace the old ones. Number four, purchase a reinforced steel cabinet for storage of restricted medical supplies, and develop a computerized program to track the inventory. Number five, install defibrillator units and crash carts on both floors. Number six, purchase step-on waste cans that meet federal flammability standards and post instructions for disposal of waste, in accordance with universal precautions guidelines." He looked up briefly. "Shall I continue?"

"No."

"I'm glad you understand. Because, nowhere in this report does it mention multicolored lab coats!"

"Okay." She looked at Jordan. He hadn't been too worried about Marlene either. Was she the only one affected? Was he always so businesslike or just that way with her? She doubted he even noticed she was a woman. He said that business was like a seduction. She wondered what would happen if she tried some of his advice.

"Please refer back to the approved plan. Just put any other suggestions in a report and I'll address them one at a time."

She stood. "There's a lot to consider."

"I'm prepared."

She went to the door and opened it, then turned to him. "It will be a lot of work." She held out her hand.

He took it. "I'm prepared."

"Good." They shook hands. She didn't let go. He met her eyes; she smiled.

"Are you scared?" she asked.

His gaze didn't waver. "Should I be?"

"Depends on what you're afraid of."

"I don't scare easily."

She let his hand go. "That's good to know." She turned on her heel. "See you tomorrow."

Jordan stood in the middle of the door and watched her leave, flexing his hand as though trying to forget the feeling of her touch. He glanced at Marlene then Emma and Peter who were waiting in the reception area. He nodded then closed the door.

Emma caught Marlene's eye after Jordan disappeared into his office. The two women giggled.

"She's perfect," Emma said.

"I think he knows it," Marlene replied.

"And is trying not to."

The phone rang and Marlene answered. Emma looked at her watch and sighed. It seemed Ray wouldn't be back soon. She stood and looked at Peter. "I guess your dad's not coming soon." She left the reception area and turned the corner. She saw Ray coming down the corridor, flipping through a stack of papers. Her heart accelerated at the sight of him.

He glanced up, at first surprised, then annoyed. "What are you doing here?"

"I thought we could have lunch together."

"You should have called first."

"I wanted it to be a surprise."

"I don't have room for surprises."

She touched his arm, fleetingly. "Ray, please."

He glanced around and lowered his voice. "Emma. Not here. I'll see you at home." He walked past her.

She grabbed his arm. "Could you at least make an effort to fit us in every once in a while?"

"Us?" He looked down and saw Peter. "What's he doing here?"

"It was a half day at his school."

"Teacher's meeting," Peter said.

Ray hesitated. "Make it another time. I have things to do."

"I met the consultant," she said following him back into the reception area.

He stopped and turned. "So?"

"She's very attractive. I'm surprised you left that tidbit out."

"I didn't notice."

"That's not like you."

Charles came around the corner. "Peter, Emma, this is a nice surprise."

"Only to some," she muttered low enough for Ray to hear. He frowned, but said nothing. "We're going to get some lunch. Excuse us."

"Don't rush off yet," Charles ordered.

Jordan came out of his office and handed Marlene a folder. "Make copies of these for me, please." He looked at Charles. "I thought it was you."

"Yep. You can't keep me away." He looked down at Peter. "Hello there." He punched him in the arm. "Don't wince. A man never shows pain. How old are you now? Ten?"

Emma pulled Peter closer to her side. "He's eight."

Charles looked at her with a thin layer of disgust. "Stop coddling him. Let him answer for himself. He needs to learn to speak up, otherwise people will think he's weak." He looked at Peter whose gaze remained on the ground. "Look at me."

Peter raised his gaze.

"Tell me your age."

He swallowed. "I'm eight."

Charles lifted his brows, surprised. "Only eight? Well, a big boy has to be strong." He punched him in the arm again. "I said don't wince. Still drawing those silly pictures?"

Emma spoke up. "They are not silly."

He ignored her. "Peter, I asked you a question."

"Yes," Peter said.

"I guess every boy needs a hobby." He punched him again. "Good, that's better," he said pleased Peter didn't wince.

"Leave him alone, Dad," Jordan said.

"He's got to learn to be tough." He poked him in the shoulder. "Stand his ground."

Jordan's tone hardened. "I said leave him alone."

"Why?" Charles sent Ray a significant look, daring him to speak. Ray shoved his hands in his pocket. "His father doesn't mind." Charles flashed an ugly smile then returned his gaze to Jordan. "And you aren't his father."

"No, I'm not," Jordan said. "But try punching me in the shoulder and we'll see who winces."

Charles laughed at the threat and turned to Peter. "See boy? That's how you want to be. Like your uncle Jordan. Otherwise people trample all over you or worse, show you up." He walked up to Ray and hit him hard in the chest. "Come on, I have a few things I want to talk to you about." He went into Ray's office.

"I'll be right there," Ray called after him. He walked up to Peter and pressed his face close. He saw tears swimming in his son's eyes. In a low warning voice he said, "You let one tear fall and you'll have them running faster real soon." He straightened and sent Emma a dirty look. "Take him home."

"Ray—"

"Now."

She took Peter's hand and left.

Jordan watched them go, then leaned against the door frame and folded his arms. "Why not just kick him? It will be less painful that way."

Ray spun around and pierced him with a glare. "Don't you ever shame me in front of my boy again."

"I wouldn't have to if you learned how to open your mouth. How long were you going to let Dad hit him?"

"Until I thought he should stop."

"I forgot. I bet you weren't thinking at all. You usually let Dad do that for you."

Ray smiled, unoffended. "You don't know anything. This is the Taylor way, but you wouldn't know much about that."

"He's just a kid."

"He needs to grow a thick skin."

"Right," Jordan scoffed. "Because the way Dad reared you worked *so* well."

"The lesson Peter needs to learn is that you have to be strong to take the beatings life gives you."

"And what do you know about beatings?"

Ray grinned. "I know how to avoid them."

Jordan stiffened; he hadn't been so lucky.

"I'll mold Peter into the man he needs to be."

"You'll break him."

Charles came out of Ray's office. "If you two ladies are finished, I'd like to get to business."

Jordan gave him a dirty look. "Looks like the old woman wants you." He bowed to Charles. "Don't worry *Miss*, we're done here." He backed into his office and closed the door.

Ray followed his father into his office and shut the door. "What are you doing here?" Ray asked.

"Curiosity. I hoped I could meet the consultant."

"I'm meeting with her for lunch. You could come."

"No, three's a crowd."

"You shouldn't needle Peter."

Charles leaned back. "What's wrong with Emma?"

"What do you mean?"

"She looks unhappy."

He sat behind his desk. "She's feeling a little neglected."

"I told you to keep her busy. A busy woman is a happy woman."

"How am I supposed to do that?"

"Give her another baby to look after." Charles glanced at Peter's picture on the desk then looked away. "Perhaps you'll have a son next time." He stood. "I'll talk to you later." Charles left Ray's office and headed to the atrium on the other side of the building that provided a breathtaking view of the Institute's land. He noticed an attractive woman speaking to three faculty members. They stared at her, spellbound. When they saw him they quickly fell away.

"You must be Ms. Ajani," Charles said, approaching her with guarded interest.

"Yes, I am."

"I'm Charles Taylor."

She held out her hand. "It's a pleasure to meet you."

He clasped her hand in both of his and smiled. "Maybe. I'm not the one who hired you." He measured the length of her. "As always, Jordan has impeccable taste."

Dawn jerked her hand free. "Thank you."

"So you're meeting with Ray for lunch tomorrow?"

"Yes."

"Good. Leave your options open." He sent her a suggestive look then walked away.

Chapter 10

Dawn hated to admit that she didn't like Charles Taylor; it hurt her even more to think that she didn't like his son Ray either. Jordan wasn't like either man. Behind his kind smile, Charles had a ruthless character. She could sense it. While Ray had a desperate hunger to impress people, she knew instinctively he would crush anyone who got in his way.

The restaurant he'd invited her to sat on the top of a pricey office complex high over the city, with china dishes, tables with marble inlay and a piano player.

The place held an easy elegance, but she felt uncomfortable in Ray's presence. He was less of an enigma than Jordan but his cool, composed demeanor hid something she didn't trust.

Halfway through lunch after polite chitchat Ray said, "I heard about Mrs. Mortimer's class."

Dawn nodded. "I apologize for that. It was an unfortunate misunderstanding."

"Hopefully there won't be any more."

"No."

"One thing must be made clear. I have nothing against you personally, but I have invested a lot of years into the Institute and feel the need to protect it."

"Of course," Dawn quickly agreed. "I don't want to be your enemy. I think we all have the same vision to make the Institute a center of excellence."

Ray rubbed his chin and shook his head. "You don't know what you're doing and neither does Jordan. I'm concerned that it could lead to unintentional consequences."

"If there is anything you need us to know…"

"What you need to know is that the Institute is fine as it is."

"I'm afraid that's where we, I mean Jordan and I, differ."

He was silent a moment then said, "How would you like to make a little extra money?" He scooted his chair closer.

"What?"

"I think we could come to a little arrangement." He rested his hand on top of hers. "You can work for Jordan, but report to me."

She snatched her hand away. "I'm not interested in either proposition."

He lifted his brows surprised. "Not even if it means several thousand dollars in your bank account?"

"No."

"Don't be a martyr, Ms. Ajani, Jordan isn't worth it."

"I am saying no because of ethics."

"A lot of people die broke because of ethics."

Dawn pushed back her chair. "I believe I'm ready to go."

"Not so fast." Ray reached out and grabbed her hand. "I know about the Layton Group," he said in a low voice. "Don't pull your ethics façade with me."

"It's not a façade," Dawn said in a tight voice. "And anything you've heard is a lie."

"Perhaps. But I know you were fired. I know that no one else will work with you and we're your big chance. Jordan may not have done his homework, but I have." He released her. "And if you get in my way, I will make sure that he finds out everything." He leaned back and stood. "Now I suggest that you think over my little arrangement. It will make everybody happy."

Dawn gripped her hands then stood and boldly met his stare. That's when she saw what she needed. She grabbed her purse. "Now I know why."

"Why what?"

"Jordan is president." She swung her handbag over her shoulder. "If Jordan were to threaten someone there wouldn't be fear in his eyes." She turned and left the restaurant.

"Dawn!" someone called to her as she walked to her car.

Dawn stopped at the sound of the voice. She then continued to her car and gripped the car door handle. She didn't want to turn around.

The voice came closer. "Yes, it is you."

She slowly turned and saw Brandon looking as handsome as ever.

She forced a smile. "Hello, Brandon." She looked at the woman by his side. "And Annabelle." Annabelle had been an administrative assistant at the Layton Group. It was now apparent she was doing much more. They made an attractive couple. Like a matched doll set.

"Hello, Dawn," Annabelle replied.

"I'm surprised to see you here," Brandon said.

Which meant he knew she couldn't afford it. "I just met with a client. I'm working with The Medical Institute."

He smiled as though waiting for the punch line to a joke. When she didn't continue, he blinked. "Really? You. They hired you?"

"Don't sound so shocked. You know my skills."

"Yes, I do. It's an interesting coincidence. I've done business with Charles before."

"Oh."

"Uh…when did you start working with them?"

"I started last week. The new president has innovative ideas and I plan to help them become a reality."

"Jordan Taylor?"

"Yes."

"I'm surprised he's interested in business. That's not what he's known for."

"What is he known for?"

"You haven't heard it? Oh no, you wouldn't. He moves in different circles than you do."

"Right now we're moving in the same circle and it's business."

"Jordan Taylor's business is women. He has them crawling after him and loves their company." Brandon looked Dawn up and down. "But you're not his type so…" he let his words trail off.

"Whatever his interests used to be, presently he is only interested in the Institute."

Brandon shook his head in pity. "Still all work and no play?"

"I don't have time."

"No, you never did. You know there are other things in life besides business. You'd find out if you took the chance. I'll see you around."

"Let's hope not."

He turned and waved then walked away with his arm wrapped around Annabelle's tiny waist. Dawn counted to ten as she watched them leave. She'd done all the work and he'd reaped all of the profits. Because of her he could afford a new car and the diamond earrings in Annabelle's ears. When they were together, he'd only given her trinkets. How had she been so blind? How could she have loved him?

How could she have believed his smile and fallen for his charm? He wasn't even smart. Dawn sighed and got into her car. Then again, he was. He was smart enough to use her then set her aside. She would make sure that he would regret that decision one day.

Once at home, Dawn pulled another leaf off her dying African violet and glanced around the apartment. She used to have blooming plants, but now most of them hung loosely out of their pots. She glanced at her reflection in the hall mirror, hearing Brandon's words reverberating: *Still all work and no play?*

Who had time to play? However, she hardly recognized the person in the glass image. Who was that frumpy woman in the mirror? The extra pounds she could take, but not the expression, the bitterness. Was that the legacy Brandon was to leave her?

She turned from the reflection. No. She couldn't live in the past; her future was bright. She had a great client and cash flow. She could loosen up a little, perhaps learn to enjoy life more.

Jordan Taylor is known for women. Maybe Brandon was lying to make her feel bad. She couldn't believe that the man she'd been working with had interest in anything but business. He hardly noticed her as a woman. Then again, once she had caught him looking at her intently. She thought he was lost in thought; could it have been something more?

How was he with a woman he was attracted to? Did those guarded eyes soften? Did he smile?

She thought for a moment. He had said that "Business is like a seduction." Maybe he had the right idea. She called up Simone.

"I need your help on a new project," she said once her friend picked up the phone.

"Really? What project?"

"Me."

"You?"

"Yes." She took a deep breath then said in a rush. "I've decided to update my look."

"I'll be over in twenty minutes."

Simone arrived in ten. "This is going to be fabulous," she beamed. "I made a list of everything we need to work on."

Dawn sat on the couch and frowned. "What do you mean by *everything*?"

"From your head to your toes and don't argue with me." She pointed at Dawn. "You know business." She tapped her chest. "But I know men and fashion."

Dawn shifted uncomfortably. "Who said this was about a man?"

"It's always about a man. Now, I made an appointment with a friend of mine to do your hair. I told her it was an emergency. So she'll squeeze you in for tomorrow. We're also going shopping. I have the perfect place in mind."

Dawn's heart began to race. "But…"

Simone waved her hand. "You leave everything to me. I promise you won't be sorry."

Jordan toweled himself off after an hour swim and went into the living room. He'd hoped the laps would have calmed his mind, but they didn't erase the image of his father taunting Peter as Ray watched. He wished the old man would leave the kid alone. *You're not his father.* The words continued to resonate. He was never going to be anyone's father. It was probably for the best. Fathers usually ended up being a disappointment. He was around Peter's age when his mother told him he had a father.

"And you're going to spend the summer with him and his family," she said.

"Why?"

"Because you're going to need them in the future so behave yourself," she said. "Don't make a face like that. He paid for this house so you'd better get used to having him in your life."

"What if I don't like them?"

"Pretend that you do. You're a Taylor. That's important. You'll know how much when you're a little older. For now you have to trust me."

He had no choice. He endured a haircut and

fitting for new clothes, then his mother drove him
to his father's house. She rang the doorbell, kissed
him on the top of his head, then rushed back to her
car.

"Aren't you going to stay?" Jordan asked,
trying not to sound anxious.

She waved at him from the car window. "I'll
call you." She blew him a kiss. "You be good."

He heard her wheels squeal down the drive as
the door opened to reveal a tall elegant woman
with brown eyes as warm as chilled water. She
stared at him for a long moment, then said coolly,
"Hello, Jordan. I'm Elena, your stepmother."

He hooked his thumbs in his trouser pockets
and stared at her, uncertain. "Do you want me to
hug you?"

She held out a slender hand. "No, a handshake
will do." They shook hands. Then she stepped
back and closed the door behind him. "We're de-
lighted to have you."

He doubted it, but looked around the grand
foyer instead of replying.

Suddenly he heard hurried footsteps echoing in
the distance. He didn't know which direction they
were coming from. His heart began to race. Soon
he saw a little boy about six running towards him.
He expected him to stop, but he didn't. He ran up

to Jordan and hugged him. Shocked, Jordan stood there. Ray stepped back and smiled, displaying three missing teeth. "You're my big brother and you've come to play with me all summer, right?"

Elena pulled him back and straightened his shirt. "How many times have I told you that you're supposed to shake hands with visitors?"

"But Jordan's not a visitor. Can we go play now?"

"Jordan has to settle in his room."

Ray frowned and turned to Jordan. "You want to play now, right? You don't want to go to your room."

Jordan glanced at Elena and shrugged. "I'd like to play."

Ray turned to his mother with a triumphant look. "See?"

Elena sighed. "Okay, but stay clean."

Ray led Jordan to his playroom, a large room, half the size of Jordan's house. It was filled with large building blocks, books, a child-sized sports car, a ten-track model train set and model airplanes hung overhead.

"Jordan, come and look at my village," Ray said.

In one corner of the room, Ray showed Jordan his collection of hand-carved African wooden figurines. It included a fisherman, a man carving, people riding a country bus, a woman pounding yam, children playing soccer in a courtyard and more. Hours later Charles entered the room. He pinned Jordan with a cool stare.

"So, you're Jordan," Charles said.

The two boys stood. Jordan nodded. "Yes."

"I'm your father."

"I know."

Charles looked at one then the other. "The difference becomes more obvious every year," he muttered. "How are you doing in school?"

"Good."

"Only good? Ray always gets high marks."

Jordan patted his brother on the head affectionately. "That's because he's smart. Aren't you, little brother?"

"Yeah." He stared up at him with eyes of worship. "But I'm not fast like you."

Charles moved his shoulders impatiently. "Yeah, well, keep up your grades, Jordan. I want you attending a good school."

"I will."

He looked around, then frowned. "How many times have I told you not to show people those things? A boy playing with dolls."

"They're *people*, not dolls," Jordan said.

"Don't contradict me." He looked at Ray. "Put them away."

"We were playing with them," Jordan said, annoyed by the demand.

"I am not talking to you. I'm not rearing a bunch of queers. I said put them away."

Ray did.

Jordan watched, unable to understand. "But—" Charles grabbed his arm, pushed his face close and offered a low warning. "Don't talk back to me, don't contradict me, I can make your life miserable. You're here because of my kindness. I can be as mean as I am nice and I can send you back."

After that threat, Jordan managed to stay out of trouble the rest of the summer until three weeks before vacation's end. He'd chased Ray into the living room and wrestled him to the ground. Ray escaped and rolled away, hitting a vanity table. The table tipped, shattering the glass vase on top. Jordan and Ray quickly picked up the pieces, but Charles found them.

"Who broke this?" he demanded.

Neither spoke.

"I asked a question. I expect an answer."

Ray trembled. He looked at Jordan, then at Charles, and tears filled his eyes. Charles picked him up by the lapels of his shirt and pushed him against the wall. "I'd rather see you rot than see one tear fall. You make them go away." He shook him. "Do you hear me?"

Ray quickly blinked them away. "I'm sorry."

"Leave him alone," Jordan said.

Charles set Ray down. "What?"

Jordan swallowed, his stomach twisted in knots. "I want you to leave him alone. It's my fault. I broke the vase."

"You come into our lovely home and break things?"

Jordan hooked his thumbs in his trouser pockets to keep his hands from shaking. "It was an accident."

Charles took off his belt. "Well, this won't be."

Ray backed away, but Charles grabbed his arm. "No, you're going to watch this."

Jordan stood without wincing as Charles made good use of the belt. When he finally stopped, Charles squatted in front of him and cupped his chin. He searched his eyes then shook his head. "You're just what I thought you were. The problem with you is that your heart's too soft. You'll probably spend your life as Ray's whipping boy because you're too dumb to know better." He stood and sent a glance of disgust at

Ray. "But I prefer a dumb boy to a cowardly one. Sometimes I wish I'd taken you instead of him."

Jordan didn't move after his father left. A cold chill swept through him. He could feel his father's hurtful words implant themselves on his heart. Finally he slowly turned and looked at Ray. A deepening hatred replaced the earlier admiration that had been in his brown gaze. At that moment Jordan knew his father had broken the intangible bond between them forever.

Jordan pushed the memory aside and poured himself a drink. Kiri walked up to him with her leash in her mouth. "You're right. Let's go for a walk."

Brandon lay on a massage table in his office and groaned with pleasure as his tense muscles relaxed under Annabelle's soft hands. "You're all tense," she said.

He groaned again.

"You've been tense ever since we bumped into Dawn."

He closed his eyes.

"Having any regrets about what you did?"

"I never regret winning."

But he did regret not keeping a closer eye on Dawn. He wouldn't let her get in his way again.

Redding's report said she was struggling. She had a tiny office and few clients. He could tell by her suit that money was tight, but with a client like the Institute she wouldn't be struggling for long.

A part of him was proud that she could weather her dismissal and still land on her feet. Together they could have made millions, but she had that damn ethical streak that always got in the way. She had tried to fight him and he'd been forced to teach her a lesson. He hoped she would learn it soon; he could use her expertise on a project he wanted to work on with a new cable company. It involved a lot of money. Annabelle made his bed warm, but Dawn could warm his bed and expand his bank account.

The phone rang and Annabelle answered. "It's for you."

He reached out and answered it. "Hello?"

"It's Ray."

"Hello, Ray. I've been expecting your brother to call me."

"I'm handling this part of the business."

Brandon grinned. "Meaning that Jordan doesn't know about it," he said with understanding. "That's fine with me as long as nothing changes."

Ray paused then said, "Things may change once Dad—"

Brandon's tone became as sleek and steady as a viper. "Now, why would that happen when we have such a clever little arrangement working so well?" Ray didn't reply, but Brandon was unfazed by his silence. "So what are you doing about your little problem?"

"Well, Jordan—"

"Not Jordan. Dawn. Did you think I didn't know about her?"

"No," Ray said in a careful tone. "I'm…I'm working on it. I've met with her and I don't think she'll be too much trouble as long as I keep track of her movements."

"I know Dawn. You'll have to do more than that."

"I don't think she's the major problem. With Jordan in charge, I can't access the money like we used to."

"Not my problem. Blame Charles for putting him in charge instead of you." Brandon smiled at the tense silence that buzzed on the other end. "I'll do you a favor," he said suddenly feeling generous. "You take care of Jordan and you leave Dawn to me."

Chapter 11

"Stop being a crybaby," Simone scolded as she and Dawn left the salon. A light April breeze carrying a hint of rain brushed them as they headed for their cars.

Dawn held the side of her face. "I feel as though my face is on fire."

"Do you want Jordan Taylor's attention or not?"

Dawn let her hands fall and rolled her eyes. "How many times do I have to tell you that this is not about a man?"

"You can keep lying to yourself but stop lying to me. I know how attractive he is."

"How? You've never met him."

"No, but I've seen pictures." She dug into her large handbag and pulled out a magazine. "Go to page 112."

Dawn flipped through the magazine then saw a picture of Jordan attending a charity event with a gorgeous woman at his side. Dawn squinted at the picture. "She looks familiar."

"That's Adeke, the Ghanaian model."

Dawn turned the page. "Oh, great," she said sourly. "That's real encouraging. No wonder he never looks at me."

Simone flashed a smug grin. "So you admit that you want him to."

She flipped through the magazine and saw another picture of Jordan. "Wait. This is another woman."

"Renee Lewis from Channel 12." Simone held out her hand. "You don't want to look anymore."

"Why not?"

"He appears two more times."

Dawn blinked. "He appears in this magazine four times?"

Simone nodded.

"With four different women?"

Simone hesitated. "Well…they are different events."

"We're talking about women, not an accessory you change for different occasions."

Simone shrugged nonchalantly. "So he's very sociable."

Dawn shut the magazine. "That's it. I'm no longer interested."

"Afraid you can't compete?"

She handed the magazine back to Simone as though it were a dirty sock. "I don't want to compete."

Simone shoved the magazine in her handbag. "It's an old issue anyway and he was much younger then."

"That magazine was published two years ago."

"We all change. By the way, has he mentioned a girlfriend?"

"We only talk about business, but I don't think he's involved. I have the impression that he's very committed to the school."

"He's also very charitable. He has donated thousands of dollars to help establish three regional senior swim centers that include a certified arthritis program."

"Oh."

Simone began to smile. "Still not interested?"

Dawn stopped at her car and opened the door. "No."

"Then how about this," Simone said, placing

one hand on the hood of the car and the other on her hip. "I heard that four women who Jordan dated met their husbands *three days* after breaking up with him."

"What are you hinting at?"

"That he's perfect rebound material. You said you wanted to have a little fun. I think he's the perfect man to have it with. And maybe, just maybe, you'll end up with the man of your dreams."

Dawn opened her car door, a sly grin touching her mouth. "Now, *that* I do find interesting."

He would succeed, Jordan thought, gripping Kiri's leash. His father wouldn't get a chance to call him stupid again. He turned to continue his walk down a side street when he heard a wheezing sound next to him. He glanced down and saw Kiri panting, her little body going in and out like an accordion. He glanced up at the street sign as the blast of wind from traffic rushing past hit him. He was miles from his house.

The gray clouds hung low and the scent of rain filled the air. "Sorry, honey, I walked you too far again. I knew I should have gotten a dog with longer legs."

He lifted Kiri and tucked her under his arm. She

felt like a limp stuffed toy. "This is why Gail dumped me. I live too much in my head. Let me see if I can get you something to drink." Doleful eyes looked up at him. He stroked her coat in reassurance. "Don't worry. You won't have to walk anymore."

He undid his jacket, put Kiri inside, then zipped it up halfway so her head peeked through. He walked a few blocks until he saw a convenience store.

The clerk pointed one beefy arm to the sign tapped on the door. "No dogs allowed," he said when Jordan entered.

Jordan zipped up his jacket until Kiri disappeared from sight. "What dog?" He held up his hands before the clerk could speak. "I just need a bottle of water then I'll be gone." He walked to the cooler and grabbed one then picked up a package of plastic bowls.

"Next time don't try to be funny," the clerk said as he rang up the items.

"Right." Jordan paid the man then turned and stared out the window. The clouds had opened up and sheets of rain fell. He stood under the store's awning and unzipped his jacket until Kiri's head peeked through. "This is called true irony. I just bought something that is completely free." He tore open the package and held out a bowl to collect the rain water, then held it close for Kiri to drink.

As she did, Jordan watched large drops of rain bounce off the hood of cars and hit trash cans, echoing like the sounds of pebbles hitting metal. He shook his head and sighed. He'd forgotten to take an umbrella and knew he'd be soaked by the time he got home. Then again, a little rain never hurt anyone.

"Jordan?"

He glanced up and saw Dawn running towards him across the parking lot. Although she was holding an umbrella she had managed to get wet. The water had flattened her green T-shirt, revealing her curvaceous body and taut nipples. Fierce desire raced through him. He took several deep steadying breaths as she approached. There was something different about her, but he couldn't figure out what it was and didn't want to stare.

"I thought it was you, but I wasn't sure." She collapsed her umbrella.

Stop looking at her chest, Jordan told himself. "Yes, it's me." He looked down and pretended to concentrate on Kiri.

"Is that your dog?"

"Yes." He looked up at her. "You sound surprised."

She hesitated. "I thought you would have something…um, bigger."

He kept his gaze on her face determined not to look down. "To be honest, so did I."

"What's his name?" Dawn reached out to pet the dog then stopped, suddenly wary. "Is he friendly?"

"It's a she. Yes, she's friendly. Her name is Kiri."

"After the singer?" Dawn asked, surprised.

His eyes met hers, stunned. "You know about her?"

"About the soprano opera singer? Of course. I love the opera. And I especially love her voice. I have all her CDs. Her voice is gorgeous."

"Especially when she sings jazz."

"I didn't know she sang jazz."

"Then you don't have all her CDs. You have to hear her sing Gershwin…I have a copy."

"I'd love to hear it."

I'd love you to hear it with me. Jordan abruptly turned around, found a trash can and tossed the plastic bowl inside. If Dawn kept looking at him with such interest, he was going to kiss her. "I'll loan it to you someday. I had better get going," he said making sure Kiri was comfortable inside his jacket. "We have a long walk."

Dawn's eyes widened. "You walked here!"

"Yes," he said feeling stupid.

"Are you training for a marathon or something?"

"I like to walk."

"Well, you can't walk home in this rain," Dawn said firmly. "I'll take you home."

"That's not necessary."

"Don't be silly." She waved her hands before he could protest. "And you don't have to worry. I am a very safe driver. Just wait here while I pick up a few things." She dashed inside the store.

Jordan followed her inside. "I'm going to get a taxi."

"No, you won't." She picked up a bottle of cleaning solution and tossed it in her basket. "I'll just be a second."

The clerk tapped Jordan on the shoulder. "Listen man, I said no dogs."

"Just give me a second."

"I gave that to you a second ago. Now I'm asking you nicely to leave."

"My dog is the size of a sausage, what's the problem?"

"The sign says no dogs. Do I need to spell out for you what that means?"

Dawn grabbed Jordan's arm when he took a menacing step towards the clerk. "We're just leaving." She put her basket down and dragged him outside. "Do you always get into trouble with people?"

"He's being illogical. Hardly anyone is in the store. He probably picked on me because he was bored."

"You're just in the mood for a fight. Your face is all red."

He rubbed his chin, annoyed that she could tell. "It's nothing." He glanced up. "The rain is letting up."

Dawn looped her arm through his and grinned up at him. "You're still coming with me."

Once they reached her gray Volvo, Jordan pushed the passenger seat back, moved a box to the side then sat down. He buckled his seat belt, making sure to adjust it to fit around Kiri. He sat back then adjusted the seat belt again.

Dawn watched him, amused. "Are you ready?"

"Yes." He bent down and picked up the box he'd moved.

"Oh, I forgot about that," she said. "Just put it in the back seat."

He studied the cover. It was a 3D puzzle of the Eiffel Tower.

"That's for Peter. If you give me his address, I'll drop it off one day."

He sent her a sidelong glance of disbelief. "You bought this for Peter?"

"Yes."

"Why?"

"I thought he'd like it."

"He'll love it."

"Yes, I know."

He set the box in the back seat. "I'm surprised you found the time to get this."

"One can always find time. Speaking of time, I had a great idea for the Institute the other day."

He shook his head. "No."

She turned to him. "What?"

"I said no."

"You don't want to hear my idea?"

"It's quarter to nine. I'm soaked, hungry and I don't want to talk about business."

"Oh." She tapped the steering wheel. "What would you like to talk about?"

"Nothing."

"Oh."

"There's nothing wrong with silence." He lifted a mocking brow. "That's hard for you, isn't it?"

She tapped faster. "No, not at all. I can be quiet."

"Good." Jordan turned to the window. *One, two, three, four, five…*

"However, I don't always have to talk about business." She paused. "What's so funny?"

He covered his mouth and smothered a grin. "Nothing."

She sent him a suspicious glance, but continued. "I can talk about a lot of things. I know good restaurants and good movies. I do lots of things in my free time."

He saw his street in the distance and felt relieved. "Hmm. That's good to know."

"What do you do in your spare time?"

Something I can't do for the next couple of weeks. He pointed to a sign, glad to see it at last. "That's my street."

"I know." Dawn turned then pulled into his driveway. "Here you are. Safe and sound."

Jordan opened the car and jumped out, relieved the ride was over. "Thanks. Bye."

To his horror, she parked the car and stepped out. "I'd love to borrow that CD of Te Kanawa you mentioned."

"Uh, I'd have to find it," he said, jogging up his front steps.

She followed him. "That's okay. I have some time."

Jordan gripped the door handle and inserted the

key. "It might be a long wait." He glanced at her over his shoulder. He lowered his voice. "Very long."

She folded her arms. "I can be very patient."

Jordan gripped the handle tighter determined to keep his gaze on her face. "You don't strike me as the patient type."

"Let me surprise you."

"I'd prefer that you didn't."

"Come on. I'll help you look. That way we'll be twice as fast."

Jordan turned back to the door and briefly shut his eyes. "Okay." As he opened the door, he had a sinking feeling he was making a big mistake.

Chapter 12

Dawn stepped into the foyer feeling a small sense of victory. She slipped off her shoes then caught her reflection in the hall mirror and gasped. *Great. A new haircut, torturous eyebrow shaping and I turn up looking like a drowned rat!* Her gaze fell from her face to her top and she groaned. Her nipples stood out like two pebbles and her T-shirt looked as though it were two sizes too small. She stretched out her T-shirt, then rubbed her arms against her breasts hoping her nipples would become less prominent. "Go down," she ordered. "Go down."

Jordan popped his head around the corner. "Did you say something?"

She folded her arms over her chest. "I was just admiring how nice your mirror frame is."

He sent her a strange look. "Thanks. Um…the CDs are in here." He disappeared around the corner. She glanced at the mirror again and tugged harder on her T-shirt. No wonder he seemed so distant. She probably appeared overeager like a virgin at a strip club. Deflated, she went into the living room.

She saw Jordan kneeling at his entertainment system next to stacks of CDs on the floor. Kiri lay stretched out under the coffee table.

"Do you need help?" she asked kneeling next to him.

Jordan pointed without looking at her. "You could go through that pile."

She picked up a selection. "You should have a system."

He sent her a look. "I like it this way."

"But it's impractical. You should have a stand or something. Better yet you could—"

"No."

"You like that word, don't you?"

"Why do women have the habit of entering a man's place and feeling the need to change it?"

"When did this become a gender issue? I just made a suggestion."

"Then here's a warning. Don't touch anything."

She picked up a magazine from a stack on the floor. "You mean something like this?"

"Yes."

"You wouldn't want me to put it here?" She placed it on the side table.

"No, I would not."

"And you would hate me to touch this, right?" She picked up another magazine.

His eyes darkened with warning. "Dawn…"

"And put it here." She set it on top of the other magazine. She slowly reached for another one.

Jordan rested his hands on his hips and watched her.

Dawn picked it up and waved it.

He lifted his left brow, daring her to continue.

She set it on the table.

He jumped up. She escaped his grasp and ran into the kitchen. She grabbed a saucepan off the table and placed it on the stove. "There's nothing wrong with change."

He took the saucepan and replaced it on the table. "I told you to leave things alone."

Dawn darted around him and back into the living room. Jordan moved slowly towards her like a lion stalking a deer.

A shiver of delight and fear coursed through her as she met his cool gaze. Had she pushed him too far? "I'm only trying to help."

"I don't need help. I like my place the way it is."

"You need a little organization."

In one easy motion, he jumped over the coffee table and trapped her in the corner.

"Should I tell you what you need?"

She released a nervous laugh. "I'm always open to suggestions."

He grabbed her wrists and held them against the wall. "You need to learn to keep your hands to yourself."

"I would say the same." She glanced up and flirtatiously looked at his hands then returned her gaze to his face. "But I really don't mind."

Their eyes locked. She nervously licked her lower lip. Something unreadable flashed in his gaze, then he bent his head and Dawn raised hers. A loud bang outside startled them apart.

Jordan released her and went to the front door to investigate. He swung it open and noticed that it had stopped raining. He saw a car speeding down the street. "Must have been a wrong address."

Dawn came up behind him and bent down. She picked up a white envelope in a plastic bag left on the doorstep. "Maybe not." She turned the package over and saw Jordan's name typed across it. "It's for you." She handed it to him.

Curious, Jordan ripped off the plastic and opened the envelope. Inside he pulled out a picture. "Damn," he said with reluctant admiration. "I didn't even know she had this."

Dawn stood on tiptoes, trying to peek over his shoulder. "What is it?"

Jordan handed her the picture, then went back inside.

Dawn glanced down at the picture: It was Jordan holding a baby. "Who's the baby?" she asked, closing the door and returning to the living room.

"It's Peter," Jordan called from the kitchen.

"That's a strange thing to leave on a doorstep. My sisters send photos to me all the time, but not like this."

He came out of the kitchen with a box of stone-ground crackers. "How many sisters do you have?" he asked then fell into a chair.

"Two." She handed him the photo then sat down on the couch in front of him. "Fortunately, they take the pressure off of me. Mom has plenty of grandkids."

He held out the box to her, but she shook her head. "Do you think you'll give her grandkids one day?"

"I don't know. I'd like to...but right now I'm busy."

He rested his head back and stared at the ceiling. "Because you're focused on your business," he said in a distant tone.

"Right."

His gaze fell to her face. "Why is business so important to you?"

She shrugged. "I have to make a living somehow."

"What if a man came into your life and had enough money so that you wouldn't have to work again? All your needs would be taken care of. Would you still work?"

"Yes, because there's one problem with that scenario."

He sat up intrigued. "What?"

"Men leave."

"Not all the time."

"More often than not. A woman who depends on a man is always left vulnerable."

"Not if the man is loyal."

"That doesn't matter."

"Of course it matters."

"My father was very loyal. He loved us very much and he made an excellent living, but then he got sick and he couldn't work anymore. My mother was forced to work. I think a part of her resented him for that because that wasn't how she expected her life to be. I think one should plan for the unexpected."

"But what if your husband didn't have to work for income? He didn't have to punch a clock or have a boss. He had lots of money. Would you still need to work?"

"I wouldn't need to, but I like to work."

"Why?"

"I don't know. I like helping people."

"Instead of having fun?"

"Helping people is fun to me."

Jordan set the box of crackers aside and stared at her amazed. "Really?"

"Yes, really. What do you do for fun?"

"You probably should ask me what I *don't* do." He returned to the stacks of CDs. "Now I know that CD's in here somewhere."

"If I were to meet someone who had a lot of money I'd hope that he would accept me the way that I am."

Jordan snorted. "I don't think people know how to accept each other. That unconditional love crap should be filed under fairy tales."

"No, it shouldn't."

He glanced at her over his shoulder. "Why not? It's all a lie."

"It's not a lie."

"You're a practical woman," he said in a mocking tone. "Don't tell me you've fallen for that load of—"

"I haven't fallen for anything," she cut in. "I believe that people can and do learn to accept each other."

He turned around to her and crossed his legs. "Let's take a moment and study couples. When people are newly in love they say they love each other and will and/or do accept each other's quirks. But once they're married those quirks become flaws and before you know it they're getting a divorce."

"Not all couples are like that."

"Most are."

"Most people go for the easy route. They try to change others so that they don't have to change themselves."

"Hmm." He nodded. "Interesting point. So it's easier for a woman to move a man's magazines than to admit she has control issues?"

Dawn narrowed her eyes. "I was just trying to help."

He wagged his finger at her. "And now you're making excuses."

Dawn released a deep sigh. "Okay, I admit it. I have this compulsion to move and arrange things. It started years ago."

Jordan clasped his hands behind his head. "Have you ever been married?"

"Are you implying that no one would want to marry me?"

He began to grin. "It's a simple question, don't be paranoid."

"No, I haven't been married, but that doesn't mean I don't know what I'm talking about. I don't have to get burned to know what fire can do."

"True, but I'm sure a burned victim knows more than you could imagine."

"Depends on the victim. Some people block things out." She looked down at her fingers. "There was a man I would have married."

Jordan let his hands fall. "What happened?"

"He tried to change me. He tried to tell me how to dress, what to buy—"

Jordan nodded in understanding. "What to eat."

"Where to shop."

"How to cook."

Dawn smiled. "You dated him too?"

"I think I married his sister," Jordan said grimly.

"How long were you married?"

He hesitated, unsure he wanted to talk about his marriage. "Three years. Some people wondered why I married her because we were so different. But aside from her obvious attributes I was attracted to her drive."

"But then you decided to leave her?"

"No." He turned back to the CDs. "She left me."

"I bet she regrets it."

Jordan flashed her a warm smile that echoed in his voice. "Thanks."

Dawn smiled back, flattered by the gift of his rare smiles. "You're welcome."

"I hope the same for you."

Her smile fell. "Brandon, my ex-boyfriend, doesn't regret leaving me. I was with him for five years and I could never make him happy. At one point he made me wonder, if I had so many faults why was he still with me."

"I know. With Maxine I never felt good enough." He glanced at the envelope on the table. "And now she wants a baby."

"With you?"

He tossed a CD aside. "I wish people would stop saying it like that. Yes, with me."

"I'm not surprised she chose you," Dawn said quickly. "It's just that there are so many other options."

"She doesn't want them."

Dawn knelt beside him and began searching

through one of the piles. "Perhaps she's still in love with you."

He shook his head. "No, she never loved me."

"Don't say that."

"I once watched the way Emma looked at Ray. Maxine never looked at me like that."

"Maybe you didn't notice."

"I would have noticed," he said bitterly. "I looked for it."

Dawn cleared her throat, uncomfortable with the direction of the conversation. "Well, you would know." She stood. "I guess you're right. I'm not as patient as I thought. I'd better get going."

Relieved, Jordan rose to his feet. He'd already shared more than he wanted to. "When I find it, I'll let you know."

"If you ever feel like organizing—"

"I'll make sure to take two aspirins and wait for the feeling to pass."

She bent down and petted Kiri. "It was nice meeting you. You have my permission to bite your daddy's ankles if he walks you too far again."

Jordan walked Dawn to her car. "Thanks again for the ride."

"You're welcome."

He held on to the door; a part of him didn't want the evening to end. With her he could never disappear into his thoughts. She forced him to face truths he'd been denying for years. He didn't know how she did it, but he didn't care. He wished she could stay so he could ask her more questions. Not only did he want her—he wanted to know all about her. He suddenly frowned and stepped back from the car. That wasn't like him.

She stared up at him from the driver's seat. "I'd better go."

"Yes." He closed the car door then watched her drive away.

He still loved his ex-wife, Dawn concluded as she stepped into her apartment. *And he's torn because she wants to have a baby with him.* That had to explain his resistance to her. She had been certain that something was there until that picture showed up on his doorstep. Then the warmth and fun between them vanished. That was odd.

"You're jumping to conclusions," Simone said when Dawn told her about the picture the next day.

"I'm not," she said as she scanned through her limited e-mail messages. "When the picture came, he changed. We spent the rest of the evening talking about our exes."

"You told him about Brandon," Simone said in a flat tone.

"Sort of."

"And you're surprised you killed the mood?"

"I didn't kill the mood. It died by itself. I think there's something holding him back."

"So try harder. If he wanted to make babies with his ex-wife, she wouldn't have to leave photos on his doorstep."

"True, but I know there's something blocking him."

"Then find out what it is."

Marlene walked into Jordan's office as he reviewed P&L reports. "Mr. Winslow from the ACCTS called to say that they need to reschedule their visit," she said. "They'll be here mid-June instead of July."

Jordan looked up at her, confused. "Who?"

"The Accrediting Commission for Career Technical Schools."

"They want to reschedule their visit? What visit? I didn't know they were coming."

"Yes, they sent you a notice."

He sat back and took a deep breath, trying to keep his temper in check. "I don't remember getting a notice," he said simply.

"You should have."

His steely brown eyes met her across the desk. "But I didn't. Do you know why not?"

Marlene cleared her throat uncomfortably. "Your brother assured me that he would give it to you once he looked it over."

He sprang up in his chair. "You gave *my* mail to Ray?"

Marlene nervously toyed with her bracelets. "He was standing there when the letter arrived."

Jordan stared at her until Marlene gripped her folder against her like a shield. "I'm very sorry."

"Is he in his office?" he asked in the same deceptively simple tone as before.

"Yes."

"Tell him to come to my office right now."

Marlene left the room. Moments later Ray entered with a look of annoyance crossing his features. "What is it?"

Jordan leaned forward and clasped his hands together on the desk. "I believe you have something that belongs to me."

"What are you talking about?"

"Where is the letter from ACCTS?"

Ray slapped his forehead as though the thought had just occurred to him. "Oh, yes. I meant to tell you about that. They're coming in about eight weeks."

Jordan held up four fingers.

Ray lifted his brows in surprise. "Four weeks?"

He nodded.

"Wow."

"They just called. I didn't even know they were coming. Somehow their letter got misplaced."

Ray shoved his hands in his pockets and shrugged. "Accidents happen."

Jordan rose. "True."

"I'm sure you and Ms. Ajani can meet the deadline. Another citation won't look good on your record."

"Neither would getting fired look good on your resume."

"You can't fire me."

"Why? Because Dad won't let me? Do I look afraid? Pull another stunt like this and I will strike you down in ways that you can't imagine. Now get out of my office."

Ray turned and left, slamming the door behind him.

Jordan grabbed a handful of paper and crumpled it in his fist.

Marlene buzzed him on the intercom. "Mr. Taylor, you have a call—"

"Not now."

"But they said—"

"I said not now!" He replaced the receiver and stepped away from the phone before he ripped it from its socket. He wasn't going to fail. He didn't care if he had to work eighty-hour weeks. He couldn't fail. He wouldn't let his father see him as a failure. He picked up the phone and called Dawn.

"Hello?" she said.

"It's Jordan. There are a few things I need to discuss with you. Can you work late tonight?"

"Yes."

"Do you mind meeting around eight?"

"Sure."

"I'll call you back later to tell you where."

"Okay."

"Thanks." He replaced the receiver then cracked his knuckles. He'd have to work even closer with Dawn now, but he couldn't worry about what that meant. His brother had thrown down a challenge. The battle had begun.

Dawn hung up the phone then looked up at Simone who was making copies in the corner of Dawn's office. "I don't believe it."

"What?"

"Jordan wants me to work late tonight. It sounded important."

"Perfect. It's time for Phase Two."

She frowned. "What's Phase Two?"

Simone wiggled her eyebrows. "You'll see."

* * *

"So what's this about?" David asked as he ate his way through a row of barbecued ribs.

Jordan stabbed his grilled chicken with a knife then cut it with a quick smooth motion. He'd invited his friend as a buffer. "I'm meeting Dawn here at eight; I thought I'd eat first."

"Right," David said unconvinced. "So how is the consultation going?"

"Fine," he said absently. "It's my brother who's a pain."

David wiped his fingers on a napkin. "What's new? So you can handle Dawn, but your brother is trouble?"

"Yes." He stabbed his chicken then cut it again. "I know she talks too much, she's aggressive and pushy, but I can handle her."

David smiled. "You like her."

"I hardly notice her."

David's smile widened. "A lot."

Jordan ignored him. "She's very efficient. It's not like that."

"Which is why you're mutilating your food."

Jordan set his knife down.

"So Dawn is not a problem? She's the ordinary hardheaded businesswoman type?"

"Yep." Jordan warmed to the subject, determined to think of Dawn's flaws. "You should see her. She always wears suits, sometimes with ties." *And sometimes tight green T-shirts.* "She hardly wears makeup." *But she doesn't need it.* "Or jewelry. Her idea of fun is to restructure a classroom and draw diagrams. Not my type at all. You know how I like my women."

"Actually, I didn't know you had a type."

David was right, but Jordan didn't want to agree. He held up his hands in surrender. "With her I am perfectly safe."

"Really?" David pushed his plate aside and ordered a bowl of ice cream. Silence descended, then he glanced up and said with a thoughtful air, "She's average height and weight?"

"Yes."

"She likes to wear her hair pulled back?"

"Yes."

"And she carries a briefcase with a silver handle?"

"Yes." Jordan looked at him, amazed. "How did you know that?"

David nodded to the front doors of the restaurant. "Because there's a woman fitting that description coming towards us."

Jordan spun around in his chair. He glanced at a beautiful woman in a cool blue skirt and hot red blouse. He turned back to David and shook his head. "No, that's not her."

"Jordan?" the woman said.

He nearly swallowed his tongue. He knew that voice, but it couldn't be her.

"I know I'm a little early," she said.

Jordan groaned and closed his eyes.

David grinned then said, "Sorry, my friend. I don't think you're safe anymore."

Chapter 13

He was supposed to be alone, Dawn thought, trying not to trip in her new high heels. And despite her new cashmere blouse and silk skirt, he didn't look happy to see her. Perhaps she'd arrived too early again. This was not a good way to conduct a seduction.

"I'll let you finish your meeting," Dawn said quickly.

"No, please join us," the other man said, gesturing to the seat next to Jordan with exaggerated politeness.

She hesitated, uneasy with Jordan's silence. "Hello," she said to him.

"Hi."

His companion wore a bright smile as though he were enjoying a private joke. "I'm David Watkins." He shook his head before she could open her mouth. "And you don't have to introduce yourself. Jordan has told me all about you."

"Nice things I hope."

"I'd say he was a bit too modest. You're even better than I expected. He's impressed with your work."

"He's easy to work with. Although we have our different styles we work well together."

"I wonder what other things you'd do well together." He suddenly winced.

"Are you okay?"

"He's fine," Jordan said. "Thanks for meeting me here. Would you like to order anything?"

"Just tea."

He raised his hand and signaled a waiter. Dawn stared amazed that he always received service so quickly. She placed her order then rested her hands on the table, aware of how Jordan's leg touched hers when he shifted in his seat. "You sounded urgent on the phone. You said we needed to discuss something?"

"Yes," Jordan said. "I wanted to know…" He abruptly stopped and looked at David who wore a goofy smile. "Don't you have somewhere else to go?"

"I'll leave once I finish my dessert," he said slowly lifting his spoon to his mouth.

Jordan scowled.

"It's okay," Dawn said. "Take your time."

"Time isn't his problem," he murmured.

David waved his spoon. "Go on. Just pretend I'm not here."

Jordan sent David a hard look. "I don't like pretending."

David continued eating, unaffected by Jordan's tone. "I'd hate to let my food go to waste and we know the danger of eating ice cream too fast."

"How about the danger of choking on your spoon?"

David set his spoon down. "You know what goes well with ice cream? Pie." He lifted a hand to signal a waiter, but no one paid attention.

Dawn touched Jordan's sleeve. "Are you okay?"

"I'm fine." He sighed, releasing a deep shuddering breath. "I just have a lot on my mind."

"I know."

"The ACCTS are coming for a visit. They sent me this." He handed her the letter.

She read it trying to ignore the warm pressure of his leg and the scent of his cologne. The distraction left as she read the deadline. "Eight weeks?"

"Less. They've just called to reschedule."

"And you're only telling me this now?"

"I didn't know. We have four weeks to fix everything."

"Don't panic."

"Do I look panicked?"

"I was talking to myself." She pulled out her notebook and started jotting down notes.

"I think we should focus first on making sure that the Institute's renewal application is in order," Jordan said. "We can use that document as a guide, to ensure that all departments are up to standard, and identify any corrective measures that need to be taken. All policies and administrative procedures will need to be reviewed to make sure they are in compliance with federal guidelines and recommendations for this type of institute."

"Yes, you're right."

Jordan stared at her. "What?"

"I said you're right. Don't look so surprised—you do offer good ideas most times."

"You just don't listen to them."

"No," she said calmly. "I just happen to have ideas of my own. However, in this case you're right. We need to focus on the areas that are of the most concern, then move from there. I think that's a great plan." She handed him the letter. "We'll have to work fast. I know two people who can help. I'll call them tomorrow."

"Good."

"I'll have to find their numbers. Do you mind if I cut this meeting short?"

"No."

David glanced outside. "We all should probably head home. If it doesn't stop raining, we'll have to swim."

"Then I'd be in trouble," Dawn said putting her notebook away. "I can't even float."

"Jordan could teach you."

Dawn felt Jordan stiffen beside her.

"He's one of the best swimmers in the country." David continued. "A three-time NCAA champion."

"I've always wanted to learn to swim."

"He's a great teacher. He used to give lessons."

"I thought you were pretending to be invisible," Jordan said in a low warning voice.

"I thought you didn't like pretending. You could give her one swim lesson, couldn't you, Jordan? I could come and supervise."

"We have lots of work to do."

"Yes, but nobody can work all the time. I'm sure you could spare an hour for a good cause."

"I'd pay of course," Dawn said.

"He won't take your money," David assured her. "How about you come to Jordan's around eight the end of this week?"

"Okay." She turned to Jordan. "Is there anything else to discuss?"

"No."

"I'd better dash." She finished her tea then stood. "Bye." She held her hand out to David. "Nice to meet you."

David shook her hand. "You don't know how much."

After Dawn left, David and Jordan sat in silence. Finally Jordan said, "You know, you're not going to win this bet."

David raised his brow, surprised. "Why not?"

"Because I've decided to kill you."

"But you're terrified of water," Simone said as Dawn searched for a swimsuit.

"I'm not terrified, just a little anxious."

She examined a silver swimsuit with ruffles. "I'm not sure this is a good plan."

"It wasn't a plan. It's a spur-of-the-moment

thing. It was more David's idea than mine or Jordan's." She picked up a purple suit then put it back. "He didn't look too pleased."

"But he didn't say no."

"I don't think we gave him the chance to," she admitted, feeling a little guilty. "Perhaps I should cancel."

"No, you won't."

"He's going to see me in a bathing suit. I should have thought of that."

Simone smiled. "Don't worry. I'm sure he did."

Two days later, Simone rushed into Dawn's office glowing with excitement. "You're not going to believe who is on the line," she said.

"Who?"

"Neil Pendelson."

Dawn blinked, stunned. "Of Pendelson Furnishings the national chain?"

"Yes." She pointed to the phone. "I put him on hold."

"Well, take him off." Simone left the office and Dawn picked up the phone. "Hello, Mr. Pendelson, how may I help you?"

"I've heard good things about you," he said without preamble. "And would like to work with you on a new project we're developing."

"Great."

"I'd like to get ready right away. I'd have to use most of your time, I'm afraid."

Some of her enthusiasm dimmed. "I'm currently working on a deadline, but if—"

"I could make it worth your while."

"Yes, I'm sure you could," she said, not wanting to upset him. "But I have my current client to consider, you understand."

"How does this sound?" He gave her an amount.

Dawn's enthusiasm turned into suspicion. "That's a very generous offer, but—"

"From what I've heard you're worth it."

"And how did you hear about me?"

He hesitated. "Word gets around. I know you're working with The Medical Institute."

"How?"

"I'm a busy man," he said with growing impatience. "I hear things all the time. I don't remember how I heard about you, just that I did. Now do you want my business or not?"

"I'm sorry," Dawn said trying to sound sincere. "But I can't right now. But please consider me for any projects you may have in the future."

Pendelson said a brief goodbye, then hung up. Dawn set the receiver down with a firm click.

Simone stared at her. "What was that about?"

"I'm about to find out," Dawn said, dialing Brandon's direct line.

"Layton," he said.

"I want you to stay out of my life," Dawn said. "No more private investigators and no more recommendations."

She could almost hear him shrug. "I was curious about you. Besides, I'm so busy with projects, I thought I would throw a little business your way."

"I don't need your help."

"Yes, you do. You just stepped into a minefield and you don't know it."

"What are you talking about?"

"The Institute. You want to restructure the school, but don't dig too deep or you'll hit some skeletons the Taylors have buried."

"Jordan—"

"Doesn't know anything," Brandon said with scorn. "He's a bored pretty boy trying to impress his father. And he's using you to do it."

Dawn spoke softly, anger filling every word. "Stay out of my life."

"I will, Dawn," he promised. "As long as you stay out of mine."

* * *

"I thought you couldn't eat anything before swimming," David said as Jordan sat in the kitchen and peeled an orange.

"That's a myth," he said and glanced at the clock. Dawn would arrive for her swimming lesson soon.

He did not look forward to it. The last few evenings working with Dawn had been torturous. She insisted on working at his place so that he could feed Kiri on time and take her on her walks. She remembered to pick up the things for Kiri he'd forgotten to buy like doggie toys and a sturdy dog bowl to replace the saucer he'd been using. And Kiri adored her, rushing to the door every time someone knocked.

To his annoyance he was beginning to act the same way. He anticipated Dawn's every visit. After he got her to stop trying to organize things, he realized he liked having her around. She was easy to talk to and they shared the same ideas. Although he paid for dinner, she always brought dessert. Home-cooked zucchini nut bread, strudel, muffins, donuts. Recently any time he thought about a donut he imagined Dawn licking the sugar off her lower lip.

"Nervous?" David asked.

"No. You're trying to trip me up, but it won't work. I can be professional about this."

"I'm trying to help you out. I can tell that she likes you and you don't want her to think that you're ignoring her. At least you'll get a chance to tell her to lie on her back."

"Are you sure he's all right?" Dawn asked, looking at David who sat at the edge of the pool with his palm against his right eye.

"He's fine," Jordan assured her.

She turned her gaze back to him, which wasn't hard to do. She'd been trying not to stare since they'd entered the pool. He wore a white T-shirt that seemed to accentuate his muscles and a pair of low-hanging trunks. Being a little out of shape, standing next to his hard body, she felt like a soft dough girl in her one piece turquoise swimsuit. Fortunately, it drew attention to her legs and chest and camouflaged the flaws in between.

"Now just lie back." He pointed at David. "One snicker from you, Watkins and you'll be swallowing water in a minute."

David straightened his features.

Dawn looked at Jordan, anxiety creeping into her gaze. "He's laughing at me, isn't he? You don't have to lie. I think he was laughing at me in the restaurant too."

His gaze fell to her face and his expression

softened. It made her skin tingle. "No, he wasn't laughing at you. He was laughing at me."

"Why?"

"It's a long story." He put one hand under her back and lifted her legs with the other. "Don't be stiff. Relax. Pretend you're lounging on a chair. Don't fight the water. That's good."

She couldn't relax with him talking to her so gently and his large palm at the base of her spine.

"Close your eyes."

She did.

"So you never learned to swim?"

"Not really well. I never found the time. I can tread water a little and perhaps doggy paddle, but I always wanted to learn how to float."

"Well, you're doing it now."

"Really?"

"Yes."

She swallowed, her heart beating fast in her chest. "Are you going to let go?"

"I already did."

Her eyes flew open and she went under. She flailed around searching for something to grab. Finding nothing, she fought harder to reach the surface.

Jordan grabbed her around the waist and lifted her out of the water over his shoulder. "Stop struggling," he ordered. When she did, he lowered her into the cradle of his arms and gently said, "You're okay."

She wrapped her arms around his neck and fought to control her breathing. Then her fear turned to anger. "Why did you let go? You left me floating without any support. I could have drowned!"

For some reason he found her outrage amusing. "Dawn, all you had to do was stand up." He gently let her go until her feet touched the ground. The water reached her chin. "See?"

Heat flooded her face. She couldn't face him and ducked under the water.

He lifted her up again. When she reached the surface she covered her face. "I am such an idiot," she moaned.

"No, you're not. You were just afraid. You have to trust me." He removed her hands, but she held her head down and closed her eyes. "Dawn, look at me."

She shook her head. "I can't."

"Yes, you can."

She met his gaze, expecting to see a mocking glint there, but it was tender, melting into hers. "I'd never let you drown. Do you believe me?"

She bit her lip and nodded.

"Lesson number one, you must not panic. If you panic, you'll sink. You have to respect water. You cannot control it." He put his hand on her back and lifted her legs again.

"Now I want you to relax."

"I don't think—"

"Stop thinking."

"But just one thing—"

"Shut up, Dawn, and relax."

She took a deep breath, then slowly felt her worries fall away. She began to relax. "I'm floating."

"All by yourself." He put his hand under her back when she started to sink. "Don't think about it. You're doing fine."

She stared up at him and suddenly something between them changed. She saw an unexpected vulnerability in his eyes that awakened a gentle yearning in her.

"Good job, Dawn!"

Startled by David's voice, she sank, then came up sputtering. She wiped water from her face.

"Sorry," David said. "I didn't mean to scare you."

"That's okay."

"You did very well," Jordan said.

"I had a good teacher." She took a step back. "I guess I should go change."

"Yes."

She walked up the pool steps. "Thanks again."

He rested his arms on the edge of the pool and watched her. "You're welcome."

Once Dawn was out of hearing, David squatted in front of Jordan. "You can't get out of the water yet, can you?"

Jordan grabbed him by the collar and yanked him in.

The next day Dawn decided to stop by Emma and Peter's to drop off the puzzle she had bought for him.

"It's so nice of you to come," Emma said, inviting Dawn inside. "Unfortunately, Peter's not here, but please stay for refreshments." She went to the kitchen. "Lorraine, this is Dawn Ajani. She is working with Jordan at the Institute."

Lorraine nodded. "Nice to meet you."

"Will you please have some refreshments for us in the sunroom?"

"I'm sorry," Lorraine said crisply. "But I am running errands before I prepare for dinner."

Emma wrung her hands. "It doesn't have to be anything fancy."

"I'm sorry, Mrs. Taylor."

"I doubt it," Dawn said.

Lorraine sent her a look, but didn't reply.

Emma rubbed her hands against her skirt. "Well, if you must go, I guess that's okay."

"Or perhaps you'll need to find help who isn't so busy," Dawn mumbled as Lorraine removed her apron.

Lorraine folded her apron over a chair and addressed Emma. "I'll be back shortly."

Lorraine left the kitchen without sparing them a glance.

"You should get rid of that one," Dawn said.

"Shh! She might hear you."

"So what?"

"She's an excellent chef."

"With a bad attitude. In the world of business you hire for attitude, not skill. I suggest you run your household in the same way."

Emma flashed a weary smile. "I guess I don't run it very well."

"You can learn."

"She's very loyal to Ray."

"That's not enough. Imagine if this were a corporation. Would a vice president tolerate a rude subordinate?"

Emma clasped her hands together. "No, but Ray—"

"This isn't about Ray. You're the head of this household and you should demand respect."

"I didn't grow up living like this."

Dawn rested against the counter and picked up a handful of grapes from the fruit bowl. "Emma, I didn't either, but I can assure you that if I married well, my help wouldn't make me feel bad." She popped a grape in her mouth. "You deserve to be here. You need to claim this place as your home." She ate another grape then pointed at her. "And your first lesson is to find us a snack."

"Wouldn't you like to wait until Lorraine comes back?"

"No."

She looked nervously at Dawn. "She doesn't like people to mess around in her kitchen."

Dawn held her ear. "*Whose* kitchen?"

"My kitchen," she whispered.

Dawn turned her ear towards her. "I can't hear you."

She raised her voice. "My kitchen."

"Good." She opened the fridge. "Ah, melon." She took it out and set it on the counter. "Find some dishes."

Emma hesitated. "Do you think it's wise to upset a chef? She could do something to our food."

"If you feel a twinge of indigestion, fire her."

Emma laughed and opened a cupboard. "I wish I were as bold as you."

"You don't have to be bold, Emma. You need to know your rights." She lifted a knife. "Whose is this?"

"Mine."

She lifted a cutting board. "And this?"

"It's mine."

She picked up a trivet with a watercolor of the Institute and Charles.

"Those are Ray's."

Dawn set it back down. "Good. I was hoping you wouldn't claim it."

Emma giggled, then grabbed dishes and utensils. She stacked them then went into the sunroom.

Dawn stayed in the kitchen, cutting up the melon.

"What are you doing here?" Ray asked amazed.

"Visiting Emma," Dawn replied without turning around.

He walked up behind her and studied her activity with interest. "You're pretty good at this. We could always use the extra help." He placed a hand on her bottom.

Dawn stopped chopping and said in a low voice. "You either behave like a man or I'll neuter you like a dog."

He quickly removed his hand.

Emma entered the kitchen. "Hello, Ray, would you like to join us in the sunroom?"

"Do I look like I have the time?"

"I just thought—"

"The answer is no."

Dawn opened her mouth to make a caustic comment then caught the look of longing and hurt in Emma eyes.

"I loved a man once," Dawn said, placing the melon slices onto a plate. "And my biggest regret was that I gave up my dignity and my self-respect to support him and he left me anyway."

Emma turned to her, her lower lip trembling. "Am I a fool to love him?"

"No, not only should you be a queen of your house. You should be a queen of your life. Would a queen let someone treat her like that?"

"No."

"You don't need to change. You just need to know that you deserve respect. Ask for what you need. Demand it and get whatever help you need." Dawn wished she had followed her own advice with Brandon.

Jordan set Kiri's dog bowl down then swore when he heard the doorbell. He opened the door ready to say something rude when he saw Emma. "Hello, beautiful," he said, opening the door wider. "What's wrong?"

She stepped inside the foyer and closed the door. "I had to see you."

He sighed. "What did Ray do this time?"

"He didn't really do anything. That's the problem. I've realized that it's not working out between us. I'm trying my hardest because I don't want my marriage to end, but I think it will anyway."

He opened his arms and she fell into them. "It's not your fault," he soothed.

"I don't want a divorce, but if things don't change..."

"I know."

She buried her face in his chest before he could release her. "No, please don't let go. You don't know how long it's been since the last time he's touched me."

Jordan began to pull away. "Emma."

She held him tighter. "No, I made a mistake. I shouldn't have married him and—"

"You don't mean it."

She drew back and stared up at him. "I do. Sometimes I look at you and wonder..."

He slipped out of her grasp and took a step

back. "You shouldn't think things like that. He's my brother."

She grabbed the front of his shirt in her fists. "I can't help myself," she said fiercely. "Sometimes I look at you. You're so beautiful and so warm and my bed is so cold."

He loosened her grip on his shirt and said gently, "Emma."

"He never loved me. I know that now. He never will."

"You don't know that."

She spun away and threw her hands out. "Everybody knows. That's why Lorraine treats me with such contempt. I'm pitied in my own home. I kept trying to believe that Ray was different. That he wasn't like Charles, but he is. When I look at Elena, I see myself twenty years from now and I don't want to be that." She wrapped her arms around herself as though the air had suddenly become cold. "Jordan, I loved him once, but every year that love dies. Soon there will be nothing left. I want to feel like a woman again." She rested a hand against his chest. "And I know that you can help me."

He jumped back, startled, and held out his hands. "Emma, you don't know what you're saying."

"But I know what I need and I need you. Please don't reject me too." She fell on her knees and wrapped her arms around his legs. "Please, Jordan. I need you."

He stepped out of her grasp. "You need rest."

"No, I need—"

He covered her mouth. "Don't say it again." He lifted her in his arms and went into the living room. He set her on the couch. "You're upset and you need to rest."

Tears streamed down her face. "I keep fooling myself that the morning will be different. It never is." She grabbed his shirt again. "I need you tonight more than I've ever needed anyone. I'm doing what she told me, I'm telling people what I need."

"Who is 'she'?"

"Dawn."

"She told you to come here?" His voice cracked.

"No, but I want to be bold like her. She said I should be like a queen and demand what I want. And I want to feel like a woman again. And I know you can do that very well."

Someone knocked on the door. "Jordan! I need to talk to you."

Jordan hung his head and swore. "Stay there." He pointed at Emma. "And don't take anything off."

She nodded.

"Thank you." He took a deep breath then answered the door.

"We need to talk, Jordan," Maxine said.

"Not now," he said in a low voice.

She raised hers. "Yes, now. You haven't responded to any of my *hints*."

His tone hardened. "That *is* a response, Maxine."

"I don't think you've thought everything through. So I've decided to help you make up your mind."

Chapter 14

Dawn sat at her desk and took notes as she reviewed the Institute's last report from the ACCTS. With one week coming to a close, they only had a couple weeks left. They would end up cutting it close. There were numerous infractions, and several major areas to be addressed that would cost not only time, but money. For a moment, Dawn wasn't sure she'd be able to pull it off. The phone rang as she highlighted areas of interest.

"Hello?"

"It's Jordan."

She gripped the phone. "Yes?"

"I need your help with a…situation. Could you come over?"

"When?"

"Now."

"I'll be right there." Dawn quickly changed out of her casual clothes then jumped in her car. What could he want? Had they been given an extension? Was there something they had overlooked? Twenty minutes later she knocked on his door. "What's the emergency?" she demanded when he answered.

He pointed. "It's upstairs."

"Upstairs? Isn't this about the Institute?"

"No, but it's still a big problem." He led her to one of the upstairs bedrooms then gestured to a closed door. "In there."

"What's in there?" she whispered.

"You'll see."

Dawn cautiously opened the door then peeked her head inside. She saw a woman in a black teddy with her wrists handcuffed to the bedposts. Dawn slammed the door shut and glared at Jordan. "Is this some sort of joke?"

He didn't smile. "No."

"There's a woman handcuffed to your bed."

"I know. It's Maxine. She won't leave until…

until she gets what she wants and I'm not giving it to her."

"Then just uncuff her and send her away."

"She won't tell me where the key is."

"Have you looked for it?"

"Yes. I can't find it!"

"Well what am I supposed to do?"

"Talk to her."

Dawn rested her hands on her hips. "And say what?"

"Say something. Anything. Talk until you make her want to leave. I'm sure you've done it before."

"Oh, thank you very much," she said sarcastically.

"Please," he begged.

That simple word broke her resolve. Dawn took a deep breath then opened the door.

Maxine lifted her head and sent her a vicious look. "Who are you?"

"At this point, I don't think it matters. I wanted to assess the situation first." She tugged on one of the handcuffs. "Yes, these are pretty sturdy. Where is the key?"

"I didn't tell him and I'm certainly not telling you."

"Okay." Dawn nodded as though unconcerned.

She turned to Jordan who stood in the doorway. "Go get my hacksaw in the car."

"Your what?" he asked.

"My hacksaw," she enunciated.

Jordan hesitated, then realized her ploy. "Oh, right." He left the room.

Maxine looked at Dawn smug. "You're bluffing."

"You'll find out in a minute."

"This has nothing to do with you. I know that he wants children. He just needs a little persuasion."

"Maxine, you're a smart woman doing a dumb thing. The fact is Jordan doesn't love you anymore. He doesn't want to have a baby with you because he doesn't want you to be a part of his life anymore. It's over. And you can't make him love you again."

"You don't know that."

"You left him, didn't you?"

"Yes, but—"

"Did the reason why you left him change?"

"No, but—"

"Find someone new. Find the man you want to have a family with and don't settle for less."

Jordan suddenly appeared in the doorway. "Where should I start?"

Dawn turned to him and gasped. He stood in the doorway with a hacksaw over his shoulder and a determined gleam in his eyes.

Maxine gripped her hands into fists then said, "It's in the bottom drawer."

Jordan set the hacksaw down and found a small gold key hidden in the bottom drawer. He unlocked the handcuffs then sat beside her on the bed. As she rubbed her wrists, Jordan leaned over and whispered something in her ear. Maxine turned to him with both sadness and gratitude.

Dawn began to walk towards the door feeling like an intruder. "I'll just leave you two alone."

Jordan pulled her back down on the edge of the bed. "Stay there." He turned to Maxine. "I'll take you to your car." He walked out.

Maxine followed him then stopped in the bedroom doorway and turned to Dawn. "You gave me some advice so let me give you some. He'll make you fall in love with him, then give you a reason to break up with him and make it seem like it was your idea. It won't last. No one ever lasts with Jordan." She turned and left.

Dawn glanced around. She didn't have to worry. She had no intention of staying with Jordan. She didn't understand him. He had a nice masculine room with solid wood furniture and lush carpeting. She picked up a statue of a swimmer on his dresser drawer and moved it to the left.

"Put it back."

She jumped and spun around. "I'm sorry," she said quickly. "I'm sorry." She moved the statue back. "Bad habit." She picked up the handcuffs and swung them side to side. "So this was your emergency?"

He abruptly turned and walked into the hallway. "Only part of it. Come on. I have another one."

She tossed the handcuffs on the bed and followed. "What?"

"It's Emma." He pointed to another bedroom. "She's in there."

"Is she handcuffed too?"

"No, she's crying."

"What did you do to her?"

"Nothing." He sent her a hooded glance. "Apparently this is *your* fault."

"My fault?"

"She'll explain it to you."

"Where are you going?" she demanded when he turned.

"To get something to eat." He headed downstairs. "Call me if you need me."

Dawn rolled her eyes then opened the door. She found Emma curled up in bed sobbing. Dawn went around the bed and sat on the side. "Emma, what happened?"

Emma sat up and hugged her. "I just made an idiot of myself."

Dawn patted her on the back. "What happened?"

"I threw myself at Jordan and now he doesn't want anything to do with me."

"Why did you throw yourself at him?"

"You told me to."

Dawn jerked back. "I did not!"

"You said I should take control of my life and ask for what I wanted."

"From your husband!"

Emma leaned against the headboard and closed her eyes. "I just…I just wanted to be held tonight." She looked down at her hands. "I know I've ruined everything."

"You haven't ruined anything."

Emma looked up unconvinced.

"Just made it awkward, but he'll forgive you. You're a beautiful, wonderful woman. If Ray doesn't see it, then it's his loss. Okay?"

She nodded.

"Now go home. You have a son that needs you."

Emma fixed her face, then she and Dawn went downstairs. They found Jordan in the kitchen washing dishes.

Emma touched his shoulder. "Jordan, I'm sorry."

He waved away her apology. "Don't worry about it." He crooked his finger and she walked over to him. He bent down and whispered something in her ear.

Dawn watched with a stab of envy as his words seemed to transform Emma as though he were weaving a magic spell. She no longer looked sad and defeated, but beautiful and strong. What was this power he had over women?

She turned to Dawn and hugged her again. "I don't know how to thank you."

"Take care of yourself."

"I will. I'll show myself out." She flashed a watery smile then left.

Dawn shook her head. "Well, that's done." She moved a sugar bowl. "Do you need any more help?"

"No." He moved the sugar bowl back. "Thanks."

She rested her hands on her hips, outraged. "Thanks? That's it? That's all I get?"

He grabbed a towel and dried his hands.

"Okay," he said reluctantly. He stepped forward and kissed her with enough heat to make her feel as though her body were melting. His mouth moved over hers with persuasive mastery, encouraging her to open it wider and allow him further entry, so she did. She wrapped her arms around his neck and pressed her body against the solid length of him. She could feel that he wasn't as indifferent to her as she'd thought.

But as quickly as it started, it ended and he pulled away leaving her mouth burning for more. "Is that grateful enough for you?"

She only nodded.

"Good." He walked out of the kitchen, whistling.

Dawn drove home in a daze. Her lips still tingled from his kiss. She felt as though his mouth had unlocked a key inside her. Never had a kiss made her respond to a man in such a way. She felt as though if he had held her any longer, her clothes would have melted away leaving her vulnerable in a way she thought she'd never be. The kiss probably meant nothing to him, but he knew women. That was dangerous.

"Didn't you sleep?" Charles asked as Jordan poured his third cup of coffee for the day.

Jordan sat down behind his desk. "I'm fine."

He shouldn't have kissed her. He should have just walked her to her car and let her go.

Charles shrugged. "Will you be prepared for the ACCTS visit?"

Barely. "Yes."

"You should have started sooner."

Jordan took another sip of his drink.

Charles glanced around. "You're starting to fit in. Ray must not be taking it well."

"Emma visited me the other night."

Charles folded his arms. "Did you enjoy yourself?"

Jordan set his mug down with a bang. "It's not like that."

"Could be." Charles shrugged. "You may want to be blind, but I'm not. I've seen her looking at you before."

"She is Ray's wife and she's loyal."

"Don't be a fool. We both know how quickly wives can become dissatisfied."

"I want you to talk to him."

"Why?"

"Because he won't listen to me and Emma…" He hesitated. "Might do something she'll regret."

Charles sent his son a hooded look full of meaning. "You like her, don't you?"

"She's my brother's wife."

"Wouldn't be the first time a Taylor woman jumped to a different branch of the family tree."

Jordan ignored the remark and continued. "This is serious."

"I agree." He pushed the intercom button. "Ray, come in here."

"What are you doing?" Jordan asked unnerved by his father's sly grin.

"It's time we all talked."

Ray walked into the room. "What is it?"

Charles gestured to a seat. "Sit down. Your brother wants to tell you about your wife."

Jordan shot his father an angry glance.

Charles ignored him.

Ray rested his hands on the back of the chair. "What do you have to tell me?"

"I think you should take some time to be with Emma."

"Right." He sat down and folded his arms. "And how long ago did your wife leave you?"

"This has nothing to do with my marriage."

"Then stay out of mine."

"If you're not careful, you're going to lose her."

"Emma would never leave me."

"True, but she still might find someone else to give her what you won't."

"Is that a threat?" Ray asked, a thin layer of malice in his voice.

"I'm giving you fair warning."

Ray burst from his chair. "You stay away from her."

Charles grabbed him and pushed him back. "Calm down. Jordan's right. You have to look after her. I told you to put another bun in the oven. If you don't, someone else might."

"Stop talking about her like that," Jordan snapped.

"Like what? Like a woman?" He looked at Ray. "Do you think because you've forgotten she is one, that others have?"

"Emma is a kind, decent woman—"

"Even the decent ones get into trouble," Charles cut in, "if you don't watch them. I don't care what woman you have on the side. It's your duty to keep your wife happy."

"You don't need another woman," Jordan corrected. "Emma should be the only woman in your life."

Charles shook his head. "That's why your marriage failed. You think one woman can satisfy all a man's needs. They can't." He turned to Ray. "Don't fool yourself into believing in the sanctity of marriage. You already lied once when you promised to love and cherish. Emma was the only person in that church who believed that you loved her."

"I do love her."

"Then I want to see that lovin' showing in her belly five months from now. Do you understand me?"

Ray opened then closed his mouth. He sent them both a look of venom, then stormed out.

"So have you slept with your consultant yet?"

Jordan stared at his father in disbelief. "I can't believe *I* was born the bastard."

Charles only laughed.

Several days later, Dawn was still trying to rationalize the kiss. She'd seen Jordan briefly twice. Once to look over her initial recommendations and when they met to agree on a timeline and she introduced Jordan to other members of her team. He didn't look at her with any more interest than before. Had it been a real kiss or a release of frustration or a passing impulse? Tonight she would see him again at Peter's school program. She had to act as cool as he.

She went into the kitchen and grabbed a glass and put it under the faucet, accidentally hitting the side of it. She broke off a shard of glass that ripped into her hand. She jerked her hand back and dropped the glass. It crashed to the ground. She held her wrist and saw a large gash cutting through her palm. She quickly wrapped her hand in a towel, but the blood continued to seep through.

As she went to the fridge to get some ice, to help stop the bleeding, her bare foot stepped on another sliver of glass on the floor. She hobbled over to the kitchen table and sat down. She removed the sliver then hopped into the living room to examine her cut hand. The bleeding hadn't stopped. She sighed; she probably needed stitches.

"You can go to your primary care physician to get the stitches taken out," the emergency room doctor said nearly two hours later.

"Okay."

"And I'm giving you a prescription for the pain."

Dawn vaguely listened to the instructions, then glanced at the clock and shot up.

"That can't be the time."

The doctor glanced down at her watch. "Yes, it is."

"Oh, no." She groaned. "Jordan is going to kill me."

Chapter 15

Jordan glanced at his watch for the fifth time. She wasn't coming. He wished he hadn't expected her to.

"Jordan?"

He told himself she would be too busy to remember. Even if she did remember, she'd have better things to do than sit on hard benches and watch a group of eight- and nine-year-olds with papier-mâché creations. No, she wouldn't come, and it was no surprise that Ray wasn't here either.

"Jordan!" Emma pinched him.

He turned to her. Soon the sound of high-pitched childish voices, and the low hum of adult replies assaulted his ears. The smell of glue and paper and wood clogged the air. "What?"

"She'll show up."

"I don't care if she does."

"At least stop scowling, you're scaring people. That's better," she said when he stopped. "I like her."

He shrugged.

"Even though she is a bit…"

"Aggravating, annoying, overambitious, bossy and—"

"And you're, of course, perfect?"

"Thank you."

She playfully hit him.

"I temper my failings with charm."

Emma rolled her eyes.

Peter rushed up to them. "Is she here yet?"

"She's probably running late," Emma said.

He nervously shifted from side to side. "I hope she hurries or she's going to miss the beginning."

"She's going to miss the whole thing," Jordan muttered. Emma sent him a look.

"What?" Peter asked.

Jordan nodded to the different buildings. "Which one is yours?"

"That one." He pointed to a large building at the end of the town. He glanced anxiously at the door. "I hope she gets here soon."

Emma straightened his collar. "Go join the others."

"Make sure to point out my building when she comes."

Jordan turned away; Emma smiled. "We will." Peter ran to his group.

Emma nudged Jordan with her elbow. "She's running late."

"That woman is *always* early. She's not coming." He sighed. "I knew she wouldn't. Damn, I nearly believed she wasn't like—" He stopped.

"She isn't like Maxine. She'll come," Emma said firmly. She held out her hand. "Now give me your program." He handed her the crumpled sheet. She smoothed it out on the bench. "There. That's better. Now you can read it together when she comes."

Jordan took the program back and shook his head.

"Scoot over so that she can have an aisle seat when she gets here."

"She's not coming."

"Humor me."

He reluctantly slid to make room. Soon the lights dimmed and the show began. An hour later the lights came back on.

"Damn, I missed the entire thing," Dawn said.

Jordan spun around. Dawn sat directly behind him draped in a huge black raincoat. He was so glad to see her that he nearly jumped from his seat and hugged her. He tempered his joy with anger. "What kept you?"

She didn't get a chance to reply. Peter came up to them smiling with joy. His gaze fixed on Dawn. "You came. You came. Did you like it?"

"I came too late," she admitted. "I didn't get to see it properly."

He grabbed her arm. "I'll show you. Come on."

Jordan and Emma watched Peter lead Dawn away. "At least she came," Emma said with a happy sigh. "Look at him. I haven't seen him this happy in a long time. Whatever faults she has, I thank her for making him smile."

Jordan watched as Dawn said something that made Peter throw his head back and laugh. He felt a smile tug on his own mouth. Suddenly Gail's words echoed in his mind: *When's the last time you smiled?* He looked at them and just for a moment, he imagined that he sat there watching his wife and child in the distance. Suddenly, a desire so potent ripped through him like a shot: A desire to possess Dawn and fill her with his child. This desire—so fierce in its intensity—tightened his groin and made his breath shallow.

He took two steadying breaths and crumpled the program in his fist, cursing his thoughts. He hardly even knew her; he hadn't even slept with her yet. She was all wrong for him. She'd drive him crazy organizing and fixing things all the time. Yet this knowledge didn't keep his active mind from imagining her with his ring on her finger, or bringing their baby home from the hospital.

But he knew what he wanted was an illusion. He knew what marriage really was. That being a father brought more sorrow than joy. He had enough examples, his parents, his brother, his own life. He knew that those you loved always caused you the greatest pain. Even if he were to convince her to share his life, how could he guarantee that she would stay? He wouldn't be vulnerable to that kind of rejection again.

He abruptly stood. "Tell Peter it's time to go. I'll meet you in the hallway."

He waited restlessly in the hall until Peter and Emma appeared. "It's about time."

Peter ran up to him and asked, "Uncle Jordan, could you give Ms. Ajani a ride so she won't have to take a taxi?"

"Why would she need a taxi?" He shot Dawn a glance. "Is your car broken?"

"No, I—"

"She hurt her hand," Peter explained. "That's why she was late."

Jordan's mouth became a grim line. He held out his hand. "Let me see it."

"It's nothing."

He wiggled his fingers impatiently. "Now."

Dawn held out the bandage; a large, dull red spot stained the white cloth.

"Did you go to the hospital?" he asked, oddly neutral.

"Of course I went to the hospital."

His temper snapped. "Then why the hell are you still bleeding?"

"Jordan, lower your voice," Emma urged.

"I probably tore some stitches," Dawn said.

"And what imbecile wrapped this bandage? It's already coming loose."

"She was very nice," Dawn said.

"I don't care how nice she was if she doesn't know how to do her damn job."

"Jordan, your language," Emma warned.

"Are you going to take me home or not?" Dawn asked.

He took her elbow. "Come on. I'm taking you back to the hospital."

"Keep your arm elevated," Jordan instructed in the waiting room.

Dawn sighed with exaggerated patience. "I know."

"How did this happen?"

"I broke a glass against the faucet."

"You were moving too fast, weren't you? Didn't I tell you that you need to slow down?"

"It was an accident."

"You'll have a lot more accidents if you don't learn to take your time. Instead of rushing around."

"Jordan, stop bullying her," Emma said.

"I'm not bullying her. I'm trying to make sense of this situation." He glanced down at Dawn's skirt. "You have blood all over yourself."

"They are spots of blood. Don't exaggerate," Dawn said.

"You shouldn't have come. Why didn't you just cancel?"

Her eyes clung to his, searching for a reaction. "Because I made a promise."

He lowered his gaze. "I would have understood. I'm not unreasonable."

Emma sniffed; he sent her a glare.

The nurse called Dawn's name. Peter jumped up. "Do you want me to go with you?"

She smiled warmly, looking down at him. "I'll be fine."

Emma watched Peter. "She's going to be okay."

"I know that," Jordan said.

She sent him a look. "I was talking to Peter."

"Oh."

"But I'm glad you know that too."

Jordan stood and grabbed a magazine, flipped through it, then sat down. After he did that three more times, Emma seized his arm and forced him to sit. "If you don't stop fidgeting, they are going to ask us to leave. You're making people nervous."

Jordan slumped into a chair. "How do you break a glass against a faucet? Can you explain to me how that is possible? People get glasses of water from the faucet every day and don't end up in the emergency room."

"It was an accident."

"She wasn't paying attention. She's always moving too fast. She needs someone to look after her. Not me, but someone. Someone who will make her relax. She gives too much. She'll burn out in a few years and then where will she be?"

"Jordan, she's going to be okay."

"I know that." He took a deep breath. "I know that. Do I look worried?"

"Yeah," Peter said.

Jordan frowned. "Well, I'm not."

Emma hid a smile.

A few minutes later, Dawn came out. Jordan jumped up from his seat.

"I'm all right," she said before he could ask. "I did tear a few stitches." She held up her hand. "I promise I'll be more careful this time."

He reached out to touch her face, but shoved his hand in his pocket instead. "Good."

"Jordan, do you mind dropping us off first? Peter needs to get to bed." She turned to Dawn. "Would you mind?"

"No, that's okay," she said when Jordan didn't reply.

Jordan drove in silence. When he dropped Emma and Peter off he barely waved goodbye. Once alone, Dawn tried to fill the silence. She talked about the weather, then how kind the doctor was, then mentioned the school program. "I loved Peter's building. Didn't you think it was wonderful? I wish I had seen the entire program—it looked very interesting. I love the idea of all the kids working together to build a town. Think of all the different skills they are learning."

"Hmm," Jordan said. He turned into the parking lot of her building.

"Well, thanks for the ride."

"Don't thank me yet," he said, pulling into a parking space. He parked, then stepped out of the car.

She blinked, surprised. "You don't have to walk me in."

He came around the car and took her elbow. "Come on." Once she reached her apartment, he helped her with the lock then opened the door. She turned to thank him, but he walked past her. "It happened in the kitchen?"

"Yes, but I wouldn't go in there."

He halted in the doorway; blood lay everywhere. She saw the telling red spread over his face. "Jordan?"

"I thought you said you cut your hand."

"I did."

"Then why does it look like you severed an entire limb in here?"

"Don't be angry."

"I'm not angry," he said through clenched teeth.

"I didn't get a chance to clean it up," she said sheepishly.

He gently pushed her back. "I'll do it." He grabbed a broom and dustpan and began sweeping up the pieces. "You only hit the glass against the faucet?"

"Well, after I broke the glass, I sort of jerked my hand back and dropped the rest of it on the floor. And because I like to go around barefoot, I cut my foot and it started bleeding—"

His head jerked up. "You cut your foot too?"

"It's not as bad."

He set the broom aside and walked towards her. "Let me see your foot."

She backed up. "I'm fine."

He walked faster.

She held out her hands. "Okay. Okay." She sat on the couch and took off her shoe. "It's no big deal." She held out her foot. "See? It's fine."

He sat beside her and placed her foot in his lap. He tenderly examined it, skimming his hand over her heel and ankle, making her skin tingle. "I'm sorry I shouted at you," he said quietly in a tone she'd never heard before. "I'm glad you made it tonight."

"Me too."

He looked down at her foot and ran his hand up and down her calf with slow, deliberate strokes. "Dawn?"

"Yes?" she said as both a reply and an answer, ready to do whatever he asked.

He took a deep shuddering breath. "Nothing." He began to stand.

She grabbed his sleeve. "Don't leave yet."

He paused, wary. "Why not?"

She let her fingers climb up his sleeve then rested them on his shoulder. "I want to thank you."

He looked at her lips then her eyes and swallowed. "No, you'd better not."

A slow smile spread on her face. "But I let you thank me."

She moved closer. "It's only fair."

"You don't have to be fair."

She rested her other hand on his shoulder. "I like being fair." She brushed her lips against his.

In one swoop her pulled her onto his lap and made her "thanks" something infinitely more thrilling. He suddenly drew back and shut his eyes as though in pain. "Two more days," he groaned.

"What?"

He removed her from his lap and stood. "I'd better go before I do something I'll regret."

"I won't regret it."

"But I will."

Her face fell. "Oh, I see."

"It's not what you think."

"Then tell me."

He opened his mouth then closed it. "I can't." He walked to the door and turned. "Rest," he ordered, then left.

Dawn closed her eyes allowing herself the brief indulgence of remembering the soft touch of his hands and the warm sensation of his mouth on hers. She didn't understand him, but she didn't care. A loud pounding startled her out of her thoughts.

"Who is it?"

"It's Jordan."

She opened the door hoping he'd changed his mind. "Yes?"

He stepped inside and closed the door. His presence made the place feel smaller and safer somehow. "I forgot to finish the kitchen."

"You don't have to do that," she said, struggling with the urge to jump him.

"You helped me and it's my turn to help you." He raised a sly brow. "You can thank me later."

He turned before she could reply. "Go rest on the couch."

"I'm not tired."

He sent her a quick assessing glance then flashed a smile that made her heart do back flips. "That's fine, just stay out of the kitchen."

Dawn opened her mouth to argue, then realized it was better he clean it up than her and sat on the couch. Within minutes she was asleep.

The ringing phone woke her the next morning. She pushed aside the blankets Jordan had covered her with and answered. "There's someone to see you," Martin the security guard said. "She says Mr. Taylor sent her."

"Send them up."

Moments later she opened the door to a short, rosy-cheeked woman carrying two bags.

"Hi, I'm Rhonda. Just point me to the kitchen and I'll be out of your way."

Dawn absently pointed. "What are you doing here?"

"Here's my card."

Dawn read it: *Rhonda Carmichael, Personal Chef*. She set the card down and shook her head. "I'm afraid you came to the wrong address."

"This is the address Mr. Taylor gave me," Rhonda said setting her bags on the counter.

"Jordan sent you? But I can't afford a personal chef."

"Don't worry. Everything has been taken care of. We'll talk about your favorite meals after I prepare breakfast. But there's one thing I know you definitely like."

"This food is amazing," Simone said, eating the lunch Rhonda had prepared.

"I know," Dawn said, enjoying her own meal. She was still salivating over the French toast Rhonda had prepared. She hadn't been able to get hold of Jordan yet to thank him.

"So why did Jordan hire her again?"

"She said she would help until I got my stitches removed."

"He got you a chef because you hurt your hand?"

"Yes."

She tapped her chin with her fork. "I wonder what would happen if you broke a leg."

"Simone!"

She flashed a wicked grin. "It's just a thought."

When Dawn finally got a chance to thank him, Jordan was more interested in the progress of the changes to the different departments than being thanked.

"Do you think we'll meet the deadline?" he asked as they went over the scheduled changes in his living room.

"Definitely."

"Good." He nodded and checked his watch. "And there shouldn't be any more surprises?"

"No, I made sure that all the departments followed the requirements of the ACCTS exactly."

"Good." He glanced at his watch again.

"Do you have to go somewhere?" Dawn asked.

"No. Why?"

"Because you keep checking your watch."

"David's supposed to be dropping something off soon."

The doorbell rang. He jumped up. "Excuse me." Jordan raced to the door and swung it open. "You're late."

David mournfully looked down at the check in his hand. "I was just saying goodbye. I see Dawn's car is here. Does her four-month countdown start now?"

Jordan reached for the check.

David moved it out of reach. "How would you like to earn six thousand?"

"Not interested."

"I bet that by August she'll be history."

Jordan grabbed the check then slammed the door. He stuffed it in his back pocket. Who cared about August, he wanted her now. "Dawn, there's something I want to tell you." He turned the corner, eager to see her, but she was gone.

Chapter 16

Dawn set the kettle on the stove and reached to turn it on, when Jordan burst into the kitchen. He halted when he saw her. "You're still here."

She cautiously nodded. "Yes."

He swallowed, breathing quickly. "I thought you'd gone."

"No. Why would you think that?"

His breathing slowed. "I thought maybe you heard—" He stopped.

"Heard what?"

Jordan let his shoulders rise and fall in a careless motion and walked towards her. "Nothing," he said as he unbuttoned his sleeves and rolled them up to his elbows. "What are you doing?"

It was a simple question but the look in his eyes made it seem like a dangerous one. "I was just about to make tea," she said, though her heart began beating wildly. "I know that we have to go over the strategy for the school once the evaluation is over, but I'd like to take a break first."

"You're right," he said his gaze never wavering from her face. "A break is a good idea. I'm tired of talking about business."

Dawn turned to the stove, unable to hold his look, the tingling in her stomach spreading through her. It reached her arms and legs until she felt her whole body was on fire. She turned the stove on and kept her tone light. "Good. What do you want to talk about?"

Jordan turned it off. "I don't want to talk at all."

He buried her reply against his mouth, hungrily devouring her lips with a passion that surprised her. It quickly melted into something much more complex. This kiss was different than before—more urgent, more untamed yet expected. This was how she imagined Jordan kissed a woman, there was to be no artificial display of affection. It was to be real and undeniable.

His lips erased all other thoughts from her

mind. Soon nothing else mattered, not the Institute, not her career, not even his crazy ex-wife. All that mattered was the feel of Jordan's strong arms wrapped around her and his warm mouth exploring hers.

"Dawn?" he said in a husky whisper.

"Yes," she breathed.

"I want you."

"To do what?"

He smiled against her lips. "No. I *want* you."

She leaned into him, a thrill of delight racing up her spine. She felt how much he wanted her pressed against her midriff. "I want you, too."

"Good." He swung her up in his arms, then grunted.

"What?"

"You were lighter in the water."

She rested her arms around his shoulder and fluttered her lashes. "Would you like to put me down?"

He shifted her weight and left the kitchen. "I don't think there's a safe way to answer that."

Dawn patted him on the cheek with affection. "Clever man."

Jordan stopped in front of the stairs and glanced up at them, wary. "Would you mind if I threw you over my shoulder?"

She pressed her lips against his throat, then whispered, "Would you mind if you went to bed alone?" She touched his neck with the tip of her tongue.

His Adam's apple quivered. "Stop that before I drop you."

"Then you'd better hurry."

He took the stairs two at a time. When he reached his bedroom he eased her down on the bed and kissed her again, as his hands began unbuttoning her blouse.

"I can do that," she said.

"No, let me," he said as he removed her shoes then stockings like a child unwrapping a birthday present. "When I dreamed of this, I thought you would be a lot more talkative."

She sat up on her elbows. "You dreamed about this?"

"Many," he removed her top and took down the strap of her bra. His voice deepened with desire as his eyes remained on her chest. "Many times."

She unhooked her bra and let it fall, a smile tugging the corner of her mouth when Jordan swallowed. "Me too."

"It's better than I imagined." He raised his gaze then met and held hers as he lowered her skirt. "So much better." He removed her panties with slow deliberation. "You're beautiful."

Dawn opened her mouth to reply, but Jordan

didn't give her the chance and soon talking didn't matter. The heat within her, which had started downstairs, continued to build to dizzying heights as his hands sought to explore every inch of her. The pressure between her legs escalated until she thought she couldn't take it anymore. "Jordan?" she said with mounting urgency.

"Yes?"

"Do you usually make love with your clothes on?"

He paused then glanced down at himself. "Sorry I forgot." He quickly removed his clothes, with a clumsiness that surprised her, then pulled her close. Dawn gasped at the impact of the heat from his body meetings hers.

"Touch me," he demanded.

"Where?"

"Anywhere."

She skimmed her hands along the hard contours of his legs. "Do you want me to do that?"

"Hmm."

She moved them to the hollow of his back then down. "What about that?"

He shuddered.

"Where do you want me? On the top or the bottom?"

Jordan stopped and stared at her. "Dawn, this

is sex not a training seminar. There is no right or wrong answer. Relax."

"But I want you to enjoy this."

He opened a drawer and rolled on a condom. "Honey, I don't care where you are as long as I'm inside you."

"Well, in that case," Dawn said. She straddled him and eased him inside. The power of emotions that followed their union surprised them both. Jordan swore and Dawn began to pull away.

Jordan stopped her. "Don't. It's okay."

But Dawn wasn't sure. The strength of her feelings was so new and foreign it frightened her. Jordan sensed her apprehension and sought to calm her. He rested his arms on her waist. "Just rock a little, yeah. That's good. Very good."

Soon she didn't need any more encouragement, the urgency inside her rising with each movement then peaking in a swirl of sensations so wonderful she bit her lip to keep from crying out.

"Don't hold back."

She didn't; she began to fill the room with the sound of her pleasure. She shifted her position until every curve of her body molded against him. Emotions so tender and new ignited with his every touch soothing the throbbing between her legs. She held him close and let her feelings take hold.

"I love you," she whispered.

He stilled. "Am I supposed to ignore that?"

She bit her lip, embarrassment making her face warm. "Do you want to?"

His hand slid up her thigh and cupped her bottom. "No."

"Do you want me to repeat it?"

He gently squeezed. "I don't mind."

She ran her hands across his chest. "You don't sound surprised."

"I'm not. It's happened before."

She paused and drew away. "Other women have told you that they loved you?"

He leaned towards her. "Yes."

She held him back. "What did you say?"

"Thank you."

Dawn's mouth fell open. "*Thank you?*"

He shrugged. "Women always fall in love with me in bed for some reason." He pressed her lips closed with his fingers. "But you're different."

"How?"

His white teeth gleamed in the darkness. "I like when *you* say it."

"Really?"

"Yes."

She trailed a sensuous path down his jaw with her finger. "Then I'll say it again. I love you."

"Thank you," he said, then he captured her mouth again this time tenderly as though trying to show his gratitude without words and soon no words were needed.

Exhausted but happy, Dawn stared up into the darkness trying to understand all the emotions battling within her. She loved him. And she'd blurted it out for him to hear. How stupid! At least the confession hadn't scared him. He was used to women falling in love with him. He'd been with lots of women. Then why did it feel as though she were the first?

She frowned. That was probably his secret. At that moment, he managed to make a woman feel as though she were the most important thing to him. But what happened when that moment passed?

There was so much she still wanted to know about him. She looked at him sleeping and began to smile. There was one mystery she had to solve tonight.

Jordan kept his eyes closed, trying to figure out where he'd gone wrong. He'd finally gotten a chance to sleep with Dawn. He should feel relieved.

Then why did he feel as though it wasn't enough? That no night with her would ever be enough? Did every man feel like this after a month of celibacy? He had a sinking feeling they did not. That this feeling was a lot more serious than he was ready to admit.

He stretched out his arm and opened his eyes when his hand hit the empty pillow beside him. He sat up then noticed the form under the covers and a dim glow of light. He threw the covers aside and saw Dawn with a flashlight.

She grinned sheepishly. "Did I wake you?"

"What are you doing?" he asked, then noticed where the beam of light pointed.

"I was curious about the hair dye."

"I see."

"I can't believe you're a redhead," she said, amazed.

He reached for the flashlight. "Give me that."

She moved it out of his grasp. "No, this is fascinating." She glanced down again. "A pure, fiery red." She winked at him. "It explains the temper."

He snatched the flashlight and turned it off.

Dawn turned on the lights. "Why do you dye your hair?"

He squinted against the glare. "Habit."

"What?"

"My mother first dyed my hair when I was five. It continued from there."

"Does your mother have red hair too?"

"No, I don't really look like her or my father."

Dawn ran her hand through his hair. "I think you'd make a handsome redhead."

Jordan slanted her a glance. "My hair is not red, it's light brown."

"It's red." She kissed his cheek. "Fortunately, I like the color red." She kissed his mouth. "No, I think I *love* the color red." She planted kisses down his chest. "Very, very much." She kissed him lower, then she stopped kissing him altogether, doing something else with her mouth that Jordan enjoyed even more.

The next two weeks they worked together during the day and shared the same bed at night. Jordan quickly adjusted to their new schedule and thought about making it permanent. He wouldn't ask Dawn to marry him, but he'd suggest they move in together. He opened the blinds in his kitchen to let the late May morning sun stream on the spotless kitchen counters. He rearranged two canisters Dawn had moved, but he was pleased overall with the little changes she'd made.

Like the special shelf for all of Kiri's things,

the drawer for miscellaneous items that she'd told him were for coupons and such. He never used coupons, but he didn't want to dim her enthusiasm. Yes, he'd ask her to move in. But he'd wait a couple more weeks.

Jordan sat down with his orange juice while Dawn came into the kitchen dressed in a pair of jeans and one of his tattered T-shirts. "Here's your paper," she said placing it on the table. She sat in front of him. "And I hope you don't mind, but I fed Kiri and took her on her walk."

Perhaps he'd ask her to move in next week.

Dawn set a bakery box on the table. "I also picked up some muffins and bagels from the bakery around the corner. Have you been there? It's great. Anyway. I already had mine so the rest is all yours." She opened the box and revealed two blueberry muffins, one croissant and four wheat bagels.

No. He wouldn't wait until next week. He'd ask her to move in today.

Jordan closed the box and stared at her across the table. "Why are you sitting so far away?"

Dawn stood took the seat next to him. "Is that better?"

"A little."

Next, she sat on his lap and wrapped her arms around his neck. "How's that?"

"That's perfect." He kissed her and was about to do more when the phone rang.

"You should get that," Dawn said.

"Let them leave a message."

"It could be important."

"Not as important as this."

"It could be from the office." She jumped up and grabbed the phone. "Jordan Taylor's residence, may I help you?"

Jordan stood behind her and circled his arms around her waist. He kissed her neck.

Dawn nudged him with her elbow. "Hi, Ray. Jordan's a little busy at the moment." She nudged him harder when his hand inched up her top. "But I could get him for you."

"I'm not interested," he grumbled, then pressed his lips on her shoulder. Dawn suddenly tensed. He glanced up and saw her gripping the phone, her knuckles pale.

"Okay, okay," she said. "Yes. I'll tell him. I know. Bye." She hung up the phone, but she didn't turn.

A sheet of ice spread through him. "What is it?"

She slowly turned, her eyes filled with anguish. "It's your father. He's had a heart attack."

Jordan took a step back. "Okay. What hospital is he staying in?"

"He didn't make it to the hospital." She bit her lip, then rested her hand against his cheek. "He died on the way there."

Jordan stood by the grave site feeling as cold and hard as the headstones that filled the cemetery. He stared down at the casket, the realization that he'd never see his father again striking him like a lead weight.

"Jordan?"

He felt the tender touch of Dawn's fingers on his arm, but couldn't turn to her. His gaze remained fixed on the ornate box in the ground. He'd buried his mother only five years ago and now his father was gone too. He clenched his hands into fists. The damn bastard.

Dawn leaned her head against his shoulder. He wrapped his arms around her shoulders and drew her closer, glad she was beside him. Glad that some of the hollowness inside him had filled up, he couldn't analyze the feelings but knew it was there.

Why the hell couldn't he have waited one week? Why did his father have to die now? If he'd lived, he would have seen all the effort he and Dawn had worked day and night to accomplish. He would have seen the Institute surpass expectation. If only he'd waited one more week. He never got to see him achieve anything. He died thinking his son was a failure.

"He would be so proud of you," Dawn said.

Jordan turned to her, stunned.

"It's true. You've accomplished so much in such a short amount of time. I'm sure he's sorry he didn't get the chance to tell you how he felt."

Jordan nodded then turned away from her because he didn't think it was appropriate to start kissing at a grave site. But he did know one thing. He loved her.

Dawn watched Jordan, relieved to see the stone glint leave his eyes and the reddish hint evaporate from his face. She wasn't sure what Charles would have said, but she knew what Jordan needed to hear. She glanced away and looked at the other mourners. Charles's widow stood supported by Ray. Emma and Peter stood solemnly a few feet away. Dawn was about to return her gaze to Jordan when her eyes zeroed in on a familiar figure weaving his way through the crowd. Brandon stopped when he was close to Ray. She watched Ray step aside and the two men talked then Ray shook his head and Brandon smiled an ugly smile Dawn had seen before. Brandon nodded then walked away.

"I'll be right back," she told Jordan then rushed over to Brandon before he reached his car.

"What are you doing here?" she asked him.

He continued walking. "Paying my respects to the dead."

"And insulting the living. You don't belong here."

He stopped at his car and turned to her. "I belong here as much as you do."

He glanced over at Jordan who was staring at them. "Go back and comfort them. With Charles gone, they're going to need it." Brandon shoved on his sunglasses. "But if I were you I'd walk away now." He sat in his car and shut the door. He rolled down the window and stared up at her, his dark glasses hiding his eyes and mirroring her reflection. "Just a little friendly advice." He turned on his ignition, then sped off.

"But that can't be," Emma said, appalled. "Charles didn't leave Jordan anything?"

"No." The lawyer, a slim, bald man with a magnificent white mustache, looked at the will and shook his head. "I'm afraid not."

Stunned silence consumed the large library Charles had called his study. The five people inside didn't move. Elena gripped the handkerchief in her hand. Ray sent an uneasy glance at Jordan, Emma darted glances between the two men and Jordan stood by the far wall with his arms folded, seemingly unaffected.

"But that can't be," Emma repeated, breaking the silence. "It can't be right." She turned to Elena who continued to grip her handkerchief as though in a trance. "It's wrong, isn't it? Charles wouldn't be so cruel."

Elena closed her eyes as if in pain.

Emma turned to Ray, her voice heated with anger. "It's wrong. Say it's wrong."

"It's Dad's decision. Don't worry about it, Emma," Ray said indulgently, patting her on the knee. "Dad gave him plenty of money when he was alive. He won't suffer."

She pushed his hand away. "It's not the same. This is horrible."

Ray took her arm. "Calm down."

She jerked her arm away and shot him a glare. "I will *not* calm down. I never liked your father, but I never knew he would be this cruel."

Elena opened her eyes and shook her head. "Don't blame Charles," she said in a quiet, distant voice. "Blame me."

Ray rolled his eyes skyward. "Mom, stop being dramatic. You didn't do anything wrong."

"I did. And he's still punishing me for it." She laughed bitterly. "He's punished us all for it. Even you Emma. And I've never done anything to stop him."

Emma sat on the edge of Elena's chair and patted her on the shoulder. "It's not your fault," she said using a soothing tone. "Charles was a cruel man. Don't take responsibility for his actions. Nothing you could have done would rationalize why he'd treat his own son like this."

"That's the problem," she replied in a tired, thin voice. "Jordan's not Charles's son." She hung her head. "He's mine."

Chapter 17

They all stared at her, speechless.

Finally Ray said, "What are you talking about?"

Elena took a fortifying breath then lifted her chin and faced him. "When I married your father I knew what I was supposed to do. I believe that I carried out my duty well. I ignored the women and sometimes hurtful remarks. I made sure the home was elegant and that any guests that entered felt welcomed. I stood by him through his different business ventures and his successes. Early in our marriage he traveled frequently and I busied myself with various volunteer organizations. I—"

Ray threw up his hands impatiently. "Mom, get to the point."

Emma shot him a look. "Shut up, Ray."

He blinked, surprised by his wife's ferocity, and sat back.

"Go on," Emma urged her.

Elena nodded and continued. "Overall he treated me well. But sometimes when he was away I got lonely. And one of those times his stepbrother Graham came for a visit." A soft smile touched her mouth as she remembered. "Graham was a robust, vital man. The moment he walked into a room you noticed his presence. Not because he commanded it, just because he was so full of life. He came to visit that day and stayed the night.

"And for a moment I felt as though I mattered. That somebody cared that I was alive and for a moment I didn't feel alone. He stayed for a few more days, but we knew nothing more could come of it because I still loved Charles and didn't want to leave him. So Graham left my life and I never saw him again until his funeral eight years later.

"When I found out I was pregnant I knew

whose child it was. I hid the pregnancy as long as I could then went on an extended vacation, hoping to quietly have the child then think of what to do. But Charles showed up and I explained everything. I expected him to leave me, but he didn't and I felt grateful. He said he wanted to make sure whose child it was.

"I went into labor a week later. The moment Jordan was born, we took one look at the light eyes and head full of red hair and knew whose son he was. I was ready to put him up for adoption, then Charles thought up a plan. He decided to claim Jordan as his own. He hired a woman to look after him. I thought he did this because he cared. Then one day he invited Jordan to spend the summer with us and I soon learned that he wanted to use Jordan to remind me of my...mistake.

"He watched you boys closely and hated how much you bonded. So he set out to make you hate each other because he knew how much that would hurt me. And he succeeded even to his grave." She looked at Jordan who still stood silent by the wall. "You don't have to forgive me, but I hope that one day you'll understand."

Jordan let his hands fall. "No, I hope I never do," he said then walked out of the room.

* * *

Dawn stared at a document that made icy shards of fear pierce her spine. She had found it hidden in the back of the Institute's last report. It was a copy of what was sent to the ACCTS, following their last inspection, and clearly showed Ray's signature. It included documentation to show that a new centrifuge and sterilization equipment had been purchased, avoiding having the Institute's license being pulled. Unfortunately, as evidenced from what she had seen on her visits, none of this had been done and with no time left, and the exorbitant cost of trying to purchase and install the equipment, she knew it would be a major blow, which could force the Institute to close.

"Emma, you're overreacting," Ray said as he watched his wife folding her shirts into a suitcase.

"No," she said calmly. "I should have done this years ago."

"Let's talk about this."

She widened her eyes, amazed. "That's astounding! You have *time* to talk? You never did before."

"Emma," Ray said helplessly. "Why are you doing this?"

"Because I don't want to end up like Elena and if I'm with you another day I will."

"Don't say that."

"Why not? It's true. I knew her story. It could have been mine. I went to Jordan one night. Yes, go ahead and judge me. I'm sure you've been completely faithful to me."

"I have."

"Of course," she scoffed. "You've probably been too busy to mess around. Well I tried to but Jordan turned me away because he was loyal to you. I want a man who loves me, who makes me feel good to be alive. You've spent your life trying to be like your father and you've succeeded."

She grabbed a bunch of trousers and began placing them in the suitcase. "You think your father was strong, but he was afraid. He was scared that you and Jordan would one day grow beyond him. He kept you at each other's throats because that's how he could control you."

"Emma."

"You have a son. Did you know that? He didn't meet with Charles's approval so I know he wasn't very useful to you. I'm taking him with me."

Ray grabbed her shoulders and forced her to face him. "I'm sorry, Emma."

"That's not enough, Ray."

"I know," he said full of feeling. He sat on the edge of the bed and pulled her down beside him. "Please don't go. I couldn't stand it."

She shook her head. "I don't know."

"I didn't want to be like him, I just didn't want to be weak. I wanted to show you and Peter that you could depend on me, that I was strong. I know now that that's not how I want to be. I buried my father and I didn't feel anything but relief. I don't want Peter to feel that way about me." His voice faltered. "I want to be there for you two and start again. Please give me the chance to try."

Emma looked into his eyes and saw the man she'd fallen in love with years ago. The tender, kind man Charles had tried to destroy. The one who used to leave love notes on her pillow; the one who would watch her dress and tell her how beautiful she was, who used to stay up all night with Peter when he was a baby and rock him to sleep at night, the one who she thought she'd lost forever.

She threw her arms around his neck and buried her face in his chest, feeling as though she were home again. "I will. Please don't pretend to be anybody else. I've always loved you just the way you are."

* * *

Dawn marched to Jordan's office as though the document in her hand might ignite if she dropped it.

She stopped at Marlene's desk. "Is Jordan in?"

"You're lucky you caught him," Marlene said. "He's almost finished clearing up."

Dawn frowned walking to the door. "What are you talking about?"

"You'll see."

She opened the door and stared as Jordan placed items inside a box. "What's going on?" she asked, closing the door behind her.

"I'm out. Ray's now in charge."

"But your father—"

"My father?" he scoffed. "It seems that my father has been dead for over twenty years."

Dawn fell into a chair. "What are you talking about?"

"Charles is not my father. Uncle Graham was." He tossed a stapler in his box. "I spent my life trying to make my father proud and the man was already dead." He placed a stack of papers in the box. "Ray got everything."

"He may not have it for long," Dawn said quietly.

Jordan glanced up. "What?"

She handed him the document.

Jordan quickly read it. "But we don't have the equipment installed and never have."

"I know."

"If ACCTS sees this they will shut us down."

"I know."

An enigmatic smile spread on Jordan's face, it made Dawn's insides turn cold. "He could go to jail."

"This is very serious. What should we do?"

Jordan pushed the intercom. "Ray, I need to see you."

"Then come over here," Ray replied.

"Fine, then I'll wait to see you in court."

Moments later, Ray stormed into the room. "What are you talking about?"

Jordan waved the document. "I'm talking about this."

"What is it?"

Jordan handed it to him. Ray read it, then staggered back as though he'd been struck. "I didn't sign this."

"It's your signature."

He stared at the document again as though trying to make sure it was real. "I know, but I didn't sign this." He glanced up at them, stark fear in his eyes. "I swear."

Jordan watched him, unmoved. "It's a shame you didn't get to be president for very long."

Ray narrowed his eyes. "You're behind this, aren't you?"

"No, you did this on your own."

"But I didn't sign it!" He turned to Dawn, hoping to convince her. "I know I've been a jerk, but you have to believe me. You have to believe that I would never jeopardize the school this way." He grabbed her arms and lifted her out of the chair. "I didn't do this."

Jordan stepped between them. "You stay away from her. You're going down by yourself." He opened the door.

Ray backed out of the room, his eyes meeting Dawn's. "Please believe me," he pleaded.

Jordan closed the door then returned to his desk. "I want you to stay away from him."

Dawn bit her lower lip then said, "But I believe him."

Jordan halted with a book halfway in his box; she saw the telling hint of red touch his cheeks. "What?"

A flicker of apprehension made her voice tremble, but she continued. "I think he was telling the truth. I don't think he signed those papers."

"Why?"

"I know he wouldn't qualify for father or husband of the year and as a man he's questionable, but I don't think he did this. It doesn't seem like him."

"Why?" he challenged again.

"A gut feeling."

Jordan threw the book in the box. "He's a lying, ruthless, manipulative bastard who worked with my—his—father to make a fool of me. To see me work hard, knowing that it didn't matter, but somehow you think he's above fraud?"

"He wouldn't take a risk like this. Why would the document turn up at such a critical point?"

"Because he got careless."

"I think someone is behind this. We have to help him."

Jordan's voice cracked in disbelief. "Help him? He has spent years making my life hell and I have a chance to call him on it and you want me to *help* him?"

"But this isn't—"

"This is a battle," Jordan cut in. "It's been raging for years and now that I have the right ammunition I'm going to blow him out of the sky."

Dawn shook her head. "This isn't you talking."

"Yes, it is," he said with an ominous softness. "And I mean every word."

"But he didn't do this, Jordan."

"That's his problem."

"But he's your brother."

"Do you think he ever treated me like it? No. He always treated me as though I were beneath him. He looked down on me every chance he could. But I was going to show him. I was going to make this institute a big success and show him that he had a big brother he could be proud of. But it was all a game. I was just too stupid to notice." He opened a desk drawer then slammed it shut. "I don't have a brother. I don't even have a family anymore."

"That's not true. What about Emma and Peter?"

"They belong to Ray, not me."

She stood in front of his desk. "If you won't help him, then I will."

"No, you won't."

The words were simply spoken, but they sent an icy twist of fear in her stomach. "I have to."

His light eyes impaled her. "Why?"

She boldly stared back. "Because I have to seek the truth."

"The truth is you're switching sides."

"Jordan."

"I see it now." He shook his head as though

finally understanding the punch line to a bad joke. "I almost believed you loved me."

"I do love you."

"But you love your career more."

"No, it's not that." She angrily brushed away a tear.

Something in the motion made Jordan glance down and sigh. He came around the desk and cupped her face. His eyes tenderly swept over her face. "Don't cry." He gently brushed another tear away with his thumb. "I want you to listen to me. We don't need this. We can walk away. I'll take care of you. I can give you everything you need. You'll never want for anything. Just come with me and forget about this."

"I can't," she said, her voice cracking in misery.

He stepped back and all warmth left his tone. "Okay."

She clasped her hands together. "Please understand that I can't. I wish I could, but I know how it feels to be falsely accused. I know how it feels to lose everything because of a lie. I can't walk away and let that happen to Ray no matter how much I want to be with you. This is who I am. I can't change that."

He closed up his box.

"But I can't do it alone."

"Well, you'll have to." He picked up the box and walked out the door.

Dawn followed him to the stairs. "Jordan, please help me."

He continued down the stairs.

She gripped the railing, fighting the urge to run after him. Fighting the urge to leave all her troubles behind and go with him, but she knew that she couldn't. "Please don't leave me," she whispered, watching him go.

Chapter 18

Dawn turned, feeling the pain of Jordan's leaving. She wiped her tears, then headed for Ray's office. When she entered, she saw Ray sitting at his desk with his head resting on his arms.

"Ray?"

He lifted his head and frowned. "Come to finish me off?"

"No, I'm here to help you."

He stared at her surprised, then said, "Really?" He straightened his tie. "Is Jordan—"

"Jordan isn't here. He left."

"Why didn't you go with him?"

"Because I believe you. I don't like you, but I believe you." She sat and crossed her legs. "So I hope you're not lying to me."

"I'm not."

"Why were you talking to Brandon at the funeral?"

"That's private—okay, okay," he said when Dawn started to leave. "For years Dad had been engaging in some…unscrupulous dealings with the Institute's accounts by emphasizing recruitment over graduation. It allowed the Institute to collect on thousands of federal student loans regardless of whether students passed or failed and ensured the Institute remained profitable. Brandon helped him with this endeavor and Dad paid him for his…services. I had hoped that once Dad died Brandon would leave me alone, but he wanted to continue the arrangement. I said no. That's it."

"Then these documents show up. How convenient." Dawn nodded thoughtfully. "Yes, that's Brandon's style. He doesn't like it when anyone says no to him."

Ray perked up. "Great, if he's behind this then I will just pay him off and we can make sure these papers disappear."

"What if he wants more?"

"We'll deal with it then. Right now we have to do something before the evaluation."

"We can't bend to him or it will never end."

"But we can't fight him."

Dawn stood. "Yes, we can."

She discovered a few days later that Ray was right. She couldn't refute the documentation and the ACCTS refused to reschedule their appointment. Finding no alternative, Dawn decided to confront Brandon. She stormed into his office, bypassing Annabelle who tried to stop her. "You're a sneaky liar," she said when she saw him at his desk.

Brandon pressed the tips of his fingers together in a steeple. "Nice to see you again, Dawn. Take a seat."

Dawn slammed the document on his desk and pointed to Ray's signature. "You did this, didn't you?"

Brandon blinked. "Does it look like my signature?"

"No, but it stinks of your dirty work."

"I'm sorry the Institute didn't work out for you."

"I can prove that you're behind this."

Brandon smiled. "By the time you do, it will be too late. Do you have the money to back up an investigation?" His smile grew as Dawn's confidence withered. "It's a pity. You're so determined, but it's obvious that you're not very good at this type of business. May I suggest you try another line of work?"

"You're not going to win."

He grabbed her wrist and pulled her close. "I have won, Dawn. I always win. You should know that by now." He released her and returned to his desk. "The Institute is going to close and your record is going to look even worse than before. And there's nothing you can do about it."

The truth of his statement hit her full force and fury nearly strangled her. He was right. There was nothing she could do. The ACCTS representative would arrive tomorrow and there was no way to stop him. No way to make things better. Everything was out of her control. She wanted to jump across the desk and punch Brandon's smug face. Then she remembered Jordan's words. Relax. She had to relax. There were some things she could not control.

Without another word, she turned on her heels and left.

* * *

David poured syrup over his waffles then looked at Jordan across the table. "I met this nice young woman and I thought you and Dawn—"

"No."

"No, what? You don't think Dawn will be available?"

"I'm not seeing her anymore."

David set the syrup down with a bang. "She's gone already? She didn't even make it to four months. What did you do?"

"Just drop it."

"I can't. Why did she leave you?"

"She didn't." Jordan glanced away. "I left her."

"*You* left *her*? What did she do?"

He turned to his friend. "She betrayed me."

David sat back stunned and shook his head. "She didn't seem like the type, but I guess you never know. Who was the guy?"

"Not that kind of betrayal. She wanted me to help Ray."

"Why?"

"It doesn't matter why. She knows how I feel about him."

"But how do you feel about her?"

"What?"

"How do you feel about her?"

Jordan lifted his drink. "She just wants to use me to help her career."

"And you don't want her to have a career?"

"I don't mind that, I just don't want to be second best to it. She didn't understand that I could take care of her."

"So she should forget her career because she can depend on you, right?"

"Right."

"That's why you *left* her?"

Jordan stared at his friend a moment then set his drink down as he realized the effect of his actions, hearing Dawn's words about why she stayed independent: *Men leave.* A sharp pain pierced his heart as he pictured her watching him leave; it echoed of a distant wound that had yet to heal of Maxine driving out of his life. He swore.

"It might not be too late."

Jordan wasn't sure. He'd never forgiven Maxine for leaving him even after she came back, offering to give him what he wanted. Why would Dawn be any different? He picked up his mug again. "Yes, I think it is."

Nearly a week later, Jordan stood in front of the building he'd sworn he'd never return to, to see the brother he'd wanted to forget. He flexed his hands and took a deep breath then went inside.

"Mr. Taylor," Marlene said surprised to see him.

"Is Ray in?"

"Yes."

"Tell him that I'm here. He asked me to come," he added when she hesitated.

"Okay."

Jordan took a seat, suspecting it would be a long wait, but Ray came out of his office a few seconds later and jerked his head. "Come in."

"So Mr. President," Jordan said casually, following Ray into his office. "I see the school is still open."

"Yes, thanks to Dawn." Ray leaned back against his desk and folded his arms. "I guess getting a consultant wasn't such a bad idea."

Jordan took a seat and nodded. "Glad you think so."

"Because of her recommendations the Commission was so impressed that we met and *exceeded* most of their requirements." He turned and sat behind his desk. "Instead of having to pay a fine, Winslow, the inspector, agreed to a 90-day reprieve, during which time we have to purchase and replace the outdated equipment we have."

Impressed, Jordan nodded again. "Good."

"And then there's this." He pushed a sheet of paper across the desk.

Jordan picked it up and read it. "What is this?"

Ray clasped his hands together in triumph. "Certified proof that I didn't sign those documents. Dawn contacted someone to look over and analyze the papers to get to the truth. She worked with a…" He thought for a moment, then snapped his fingers. "Gail Walters, a top handwriting analyst. Ever heard of her?"

"Vaguely."

"She's great. She contacted me and told me that she could prove the handwriting was a forgery. It's currently under investigation."

Jordan impatiently drummed his fingers on his knee. "I'm glad everything is going well. So why did you ask me to come?"

"Because I know you did all that for Dawn."

Jordan stopped drumming and stared at him in astonished silence. He quickly recovered. "I don't know what you're talking about. I didn't do anything. You just said Dawn did all these great things."

Ray watched his brother closely. "Yes, I know that Dawn helped change the school and prepare it for the evaluation, but I found it amazing that

Winslow knew so much detail about all the changes."

"So?" Jordan said uncomfortable with Ray's assessing gaze. "He was probably very thorough."

"And he told me that his supervisor had raved about the Institute and its new consultant. When I learned that his supervisor was *Ms.* Neuval, I just started thinking." He narrowed his gaze. "I know you, Jordan, don't deny it."

Jordan shrugged. "Okay, so I talked to her a little."

"And Ms. Walters couldn't help slip that she was only helping me because she was doing you a favor."

"Damn, I told her not to say anything."

"She couldn't help it. She wanted to know about the woman who had finally gotten to you."

Jordan stood. "Yes, well as I said I'm glad everything worked out. If that's all…"

All amusement left Ray's voice and he said, "I know that you didn't do any of those things for me, but I wanted to thank you anyway."

Jordan waved his words away and took a step back. "Don't worry about it. It's nothing."

"Nothing?" Ray said with feeling. He rose to his feet. "Not only did you save my reputation and furthered Dawn's career, you changed the lives of thousands of students. Did you know that two other schools want to know about our new teaching model?"

"That wasn't—"

"And Emma. I don't know what you said to her, but she's a new woman. You should see her with Lorraine, it's amazing. You've changed our lives and I'm proud—" He paused when his voice became unsteady. "I'm proud to call you my brother."

Jordan's throat closed. He nodded, unable to speak.

"And if you're ever in the area," Ray cleared his throat, "uh, feel free to stop by."

He flashed a quick smile. "Thanks, I'll do that."

"Mom would like to see you too."

"I know," he said in a distant tone. "I'd like to see her, too."

"It's not too late to make things right, you know," Ray said as Jordan opened the door. "Emma taught me that it's easy to forgive those you love."

Dawn put the receiver down with a sigh. Ever since her success with The Medical Institute her phone had been ringing nonstop. Requests for consultations flooded her e-mail. She glanced around her office with a proud grin. Soon she could go hunting for another office space.

The grin faltered a little. Her life had become all about business again. Not that she minded, yet there were times when she thought about Jordan and the fun they had together. But those memories always ended with him walking away…

"Dawn," Simone said through the intercom. "Your eleven-thirty appointment is here."

Dawn jumped from her seat and rubbed her hands together, fighting against the heartache that lingered. "Great. Send them in." She stood in front of the door with a ready grin. It fell when Jordan walked into the room.

Her heart jolted, but she pushed the feeling aside and nudged him to the door. "Not now. I have an appointment."

"I know." He moved past her and sat down. He stared up at her amused. "With me."

"No." She looked at her schedule. "With JT's swimsuits for dogs."

He nodded. "Yes, that's me."

Her mouth fell open. "You're not serious."

He grinned. "No, I'm not serious." His expression changed. "I just wanted to see you."

Dawn walked to the window and stared down

at the parking lot unable to look at him. Afraid her feelings would show on her face. Afraid she would shamelessly throw herself at him.

The bright June sun polished the tops of cars, warming the pavement and the people bustling back and forth dressed in summer attire. She watched a squirrel challenge a pigeon for a dropped hot dog bun and lifted the window to feel the slight breeze that caused electric wires to sway and rustled the feathers of the birds sitting on top of them. She rested her forehead against the window. "Ray told me what you did."

"Oh."

She turned to him curious. "Why did you do it?"

His gaze fell. "Because…" He paused, then lifted his gaze to hers. His eyes probed her very soul. "Because I promised you I'd never let you drown."

She met his gaze without flinching, knowing she would never be afraid of his gaze again, that she would always find his eyes beautiful. "Is that all?" she asked in a soft voice.

He stood and reached out to her then stopped.

"And I love you," he said in a tone that shook with the intensity of his feeling.

She briefly shut her eyes feeling a wave of intangible joy flow through her. She smiled and he held out his arms. "Thank you," she whispered into his chest, not caring that he held her too tight, as though he were afraid of losing her again.

Dawn held him close as well, not from fear, but because she enjoyed being in his arms again and she wouldn't deny herself the pleasure. "I love you, too."

His lips bent to meet hers and for a long moment they were the only two people in the world. Jordan reluctantly withdrew. "I've reserved tickets for the opera."

"At the Metropolitan?"

"And the Sydney Opera House."

She stared at him speechless.

"And the Vienna State and Covent Garden." A slow smile spread on his face. "Do you want me to continue?"

"You reserved tickets to all the best opera houses in the world?"

He shrugged. "You can't work all the time."

She wrapped her arms around his waist, laid her cheek against his chest and listened to the steady rhythm of his heart. "With you in my life, I'd never want to."

Jordan held her snugly and rested his chin on her head. He groaned in resignation. "I'm going to marry you, aren't I?"

Dawn drew back, apprehension stealing some of her joy. "You don't have to."

He released a long breath then said, "I know." He cradled her face in his hands, his voice filled with wonder. "I want to."

Dawn felt like laughing and crying at the same time. "I'm glad. That had been my plan all along."

Big-boned beauty, Chere Adams
plunges headfirst into an
extreme makeover to impress
fitness fanatic
Quentin Abrahams.

But perhaps it's Chere's curves that
have caught Quentin's eye?

All About Me

Marcia
King-Gamble

AVAILABLE JANUARY 2007
FROM KIMANI™ ROMANCE

Love's Ultimate Destination

Available at your favorite retail outlet.